P9-CAD-013

"I'm coming up," Miriam said.

Charley offered his hand when she reached the top rung of the ladder. She took it and climbed up into the shadowy loft. Charley squeezed her fingers in his and she suddenly realized he was still holding her hand, or she was holding his; she wasn't quite sure which it was.

She quickly tucked her hand behind her back and averted her gaze, as a small thrill of excitement passed through her.

"Miriam," he began.

She backed toward the ladder. "I j-just wanted to see the hay," she stammered, feeling all off-kilter. She didn't know why, but she felt as if she needed to get away from Charley, as if she needed to catch her breath. "I've got things to do."

Charley followed her down. Miriam felt her cheeks grow warm. She felt completely flustered and didn't know why. She'd held Charley's hand plenty of times before. What made this time different?

Charley was looking at Miriam strangely.

Something had changed between them in those few seconds up in the hayloft and Miriam wasn't sure what.

Books by Emma Miller

Love Inspired

*Courting Ruth
*Miriam's Heart

*Hannah's Daughters

EMMA MILLER

lives quietly in her old farmhouse in rural Delaware amid fertile fields and lush woodlands. Fortunate enough to be born into a family of strong faith, she grew up on a dairy farm, surrounded by loving parents, siblings, grandparents, aunts, uncles and cousins. Emma was educated in local schools, and once taught in an Amish schoolhouse much like the one at Seven Poplars. When she's not caring for her large family, reading and writing are her favorite pastimes.

Miriam's Heart
Emma Miller

Love Inspired

If you purchased this book without a cover you should be aware
that this book is stolen property. It was reported as "unsold and
destroyed" to the publisher, and neither the author nor the
publisher has received any payment for this "stripped book."

Recycling programs
for this product may
not exist in your area.

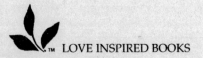 LOVE INSPIRED BOOKS

ISBN-13: 978-0-373-87668-6

MIRIAM'S HEART

Copyright © 2011 by Emma Miller

All rights reserved. Except for use in any review, the reproduction
or utilization of this work in whole or in part in any form by any
electronic, mechanical or other means, now known or hereafter
invented, including xerography, photocopying and recording, or in
any information storage or retrieval system, is forbidden without
the written permission of the editorial office, Love Inspired Books,
233 Broadway, New York, NY 10279 U.S.A.

This is a work of fiction. Names, characters, places and incidents are
either the product of the author's imagination or are used fictitiously, and
any resemblance to actual persons, living or dead, business establishments,
events or locales is entirely coincidental.

This edition published by arrangement with Love Inspired Books,

® and TM are trademarks of Love Inspired Books, used under license.
Trademarks indicated with ® are registered in the United States Patent
and Trademark Office, the Canadian Trade Marks Office and in other
countries.

www.LoveInspiredBooks.com

Printed in U.S.A.

Love comes from a pure heart and a
good conscience and a sincere faith.
—1 *Timothy* 1:5

For the lost Prince of Persia
and the blessings he has brought to our family

Chapter One

Kent County, Delaware—Early Autumn

"Whoa, easy, Blackie!" Miriam cried as the black horse slipped and nearly fell. The iron-wheeled wagon swayed ominously. Blackie's teammate, Molly, stood patiently until the gelding recovered his footing.

Miriam let out a sigh of relief as her racing pulse returned to normal. She'd been driving teams since she was six, but Blackie was young and had a lot to learn. Gripping the leathers firmly in her small hands, Miriam guided the horses along the muddy farm lane that ran between her family's orchard and the creek. The bank on her right was steep, the water higher than normal due to heavy rain earlier in the week.

"Not far now," she soothed. Thank the Lord for Molly. The dapple-gray mare might have been past her prime, but she could always be counted on to do her job without any fuss. The wagon was piled high with bales of hay, and Miriam didn't want to lose any off the back.

Haying was one of the few tasks the Yoder girls and their mother hadn't done on their farm since Dat's death two years ago. Instead, they traded the use of pasture

land with Uncle Reuben for his extra hay. He paid an
English farmer to cut and bale the timothy and clover.
All Miriam had to do was haul the sweet-smelling bales
home. Today, she was in a hurry. The sky suggested there
was more rain coming out of the west and she had to get
the hay stacked in the barn before the skies opened up.
Not that she minded. In fact, she liked this kind of work:
the steady clip-clop of the horses' hooves, the smell of
the timothy, the feel of the reins in her hands.

If Mam and Dat had had sons instead of seven daughters, Miriam supposed she'd have been confined to working in the house and garden like most Amish girls. But
she'd always been different, the girl people called a
tomboy, and she preferred outside chores. Despite her
modest dress and Amish *kapp,* Miriam loved being in
the fields in any weather and had a real knack with livestock. It might have been sinful pride, but when it came
to farming, she secretly considered herself a match for
any young man in the county.

It had been her father who'd taught her all she knew
about planting and harvesting and rotating the crops. Her
earliest memory was of riding on his wide shoulders as
he drove the cows into the barn for milking. Since his
death, she'd tried to fill his shoes, but his absence had
left a great hole in their family and in her heart.

Miriam's mother had taken over the teaching position
at the Seven Poplars Amish school and all of Miriam's
unmarried sisters pitched in on the farm. It wasn't easy,
but they managed to keep the large homestead going,
tending the animals, planting and harvesting crops and
helping the less fortunate. All too soon, Miriam knew it
would be harder. With Ruth marrying in November and
going to live in the new house she and Eli were building

on the far end of the property, there would be one less pair of hands to help.

Blackie's startled snort and laid back ears yanked Miriam from her daydreaming. "Easy, boy. What's wrong?" She quickly scanned the lane she'd been following that ran along a small creek. There wasn't anything to frighten him, nothing but a weathered black stick lying between the wagon ruts.

But the gelding didn't settle down. Instead, he stiffened, let out a shrill whinny and reared up in the traces, as the muddy branch came alive, raised its head, hissed threateningly and slithered directly toward Blackie.

Snake! Miriam shuddered as she came to her feet and fought to gain control of the terrified horses. She hated snakes. And this black snake was huge.

Blackie reared again, pawed the air and threw himself sideways, crashing into the mare and sending both animals and the hay wagon tumbling off the road and down the bank. A wagon wheel cracked and Miriam jumped free before she was caught in the tangle of thrashing horses, leather harnesses, wood and hay bales.

She landed in the road, nearly on top of the snake. Both horses were whinnying frantically, but for long seconds, Miriam lay sprawled in the mud, the wind knocked out of her. The black snake slithered across her wrist, making its escape and she squealed with disgust, and rolled away from it. Vaguely, she heard someone shouting her name, but all she could think of was her horses.

Charley Byler was halfway across the field from the Yoders' barn when he saw the black horse rear up in its traces. He dropped his lunch pail and broke into a run as the team and wagon toppled off the side of the lane into the creek.

He was a fast runner. He usually won the races at community picnics and frolics, but he wasn't fast enough to reach Miriam before she'd climbed up off the road and disappeared over the stream bank. *"Ne!"* he shouted. "Miriam, don't!"

But she didn't listen. Miriam—his dear Miriam— never listened to anything he said. Heart in his throat, Charley's feet pounded the grass until, breathless, he reached the lane and half slid, half fell into the creek beside her. "Miriam!" He caught her shoulders and pulled her back from the kicking, flailing animals.

"Let me go! I have to—"

He caught her around the waist, surprised by how strong she was, especially for such a little thing. "Listen to me," he pleaded. He knew how valuable the team was and how attached Miriam was to them, but he also knew how dangerous a frightened horse could be. His own brother had been killed by a yearling colt's hoof when the boy was only eight years old. "Miriam, you can't do it this way!"

Blackie, still kicking, had fallen on top of Molly. The mare's eyes rolled back in her head so that only the whites showed. She thrashed and neighed pitifully in the muck, blood seeping from her neck and hindquarters to tint the creek water a sickening pink.

"You have to help me," Miriam insisted. "Blackie will—"

At that instant, Charley's boot slipped on the muddy bottom and they both went down into the waist-deep water.

To Charley's surprise, Miriam—who never cried— burst into tears. He was helping her to her feet, when he heard the frantic barking of a dog. Irwin and his terrier appeared at the edge of the road.

"You all right?" Thirteen-year-old Irwin Beachy wasn't family, but he acted like it since he'd come to live with the Yoders. He was home from school today, supposedly with a sore throat, but he was known to fib to get out of school. "What can I do?"

"I'm not hurt," Miriam answered, between sobs. "Run quick…to the chair shop. Use the phone to…to call Hartman's. Tell them…tell them it's an emergency. We need a vet right away."

Miriam started to shiver. Her purple dress and white apron were soaked through, her *kapp* gone. Charley thought Miriam would be better off out of the water, but he knew better than to suggest it. She'd not leave these animals until they were out of the creek.

"You want me to climb down there?" Irwin asked. "Maybe we could unhook the—"

"We might do more harm than good." Charley looked down at the horses; they were quieter now, wide-eyed with fear, but not struggling. "I'd rather have one of the Hartmans here before we try that."

"The phone, Irwin!" Miriam cried. "Call the Hartmans."

"Ask for Albert, if you can," Charley called after the boy as he took off with the dog on his heels. "We need someone with experience."

"Get whoever can come the fastest!" Miriam pulled loose from Charley and waded toward the horses. "Shh, shh," she murmured. "Easy, now."

The dapple-gray mare lay still, her head held at an awkward angle out of the water. Charley hoped that the old girl didn't have a broken leg. The first time he'd ever used a cultivator was behind that mare. Miriam's father had showed him how and he'd always been grateful to Jonas and to Molly for the lesson. Since Miriam seemed to be calming Blackie, Charley knelt down and supported the mare's head.

Blood continued to seep from a long scrape on the horse's neck. Charley supposed the wound would need sewing up, but it didn't look like something that was fatal. Her hind legs were what worried him. If a bone was shattered, it would be the end of the road for the mare. Miriam was a wonder with horses, with most any animal really, but she couldn't heal a broken bone in a horse's leg. Some people tried that with expensive racehorses, but like all Amish, the Yoders didn't carry insurance on their animals, or on anything else. Sending an old horse off to some fancy veterinary hospital was beyond what Miriam's Mam or the church could afford. When horses in Seven Poplars broke a leg, they had to be put down.

Charley stroked the dapple-gray's head. He felt so sorry for her, but he didn't dare to try and get the horses out of the creek until he had more help. If one of them didn't have broken bones yet, the fright of getting them free might cause it.

Charley glanced at Miriam. One of her red-gold braids had come unpinned and hung over her shoulder. He swallowed hard. He knew he shouldn't be staring at her hair. That was for a husband to see in the privacy of their home. But he couldn't look away. It was so beautiful in the sunlight, and the little curling hairs at the back of her neck gleamed with drops of creek water.

A warmth curled in his stomach and seeped up to make his chest so tight that it was hard to breathe. He'd known Miriam Yoder since they were both in leading strings. They'd napped together on a blanket in a corner of his mother's garden, as babies. Then, when they'd gotten older, maybe three or four, they'd played on her porch, swinging on the bench swing and taking all the animals out of a Noah's Ark her Dat had carved for her and lining them up, two by two.

He guessed that he'd loved Miriam as long as he could remember, but she'd been just Miriam, like one of his sisters, only tougher. Last spring, he'd bought her pie at the school fundraiser and they'd shared many a picnic lunch. He'd always liked Miriam and he'd never cared that she was different from most girls, never cared that she could pitch a baseball better than him or catch more fish in the pond. He'd teased her, ridden with her to group sings and played clapping games at the young people's doings.

Miriam was as familiar to him as his own mother, but standing here in the creek without her *kapp*, her dress soaked and muddy, scowling at him, he felt like he didn't know her at all. He could have told any of his pals that he loved Miriam Yoder, but he hadn't realized what that meant...until this moment. Suddenly, the thought that she could have been hurt when the wagon turned over, that she could have been tangled in the lines and pulled under, or crushed by the horses, brought tears to his eyes.

"Miriam," he said. His mouth felt dry. His tongue stuck to the roof of his mouth.

"Yes?" She turned those intense gray eyes from the horse back to him.

He suddenly felt foolish. He didn't know what he was saying. He couldn't tell her how he felt. They hadn't ridden home from a frolic together more than three or four times. They hadn't walked out together and she hadn't invited him in when they'd gotten to her house and everyone else was asleep. They'd been friends, chums; they ran around with the same gang. He couldn't just blurt out that he suddenly realized that he *loved* her. "Nothing. Never mind."

She returned her attention to Blackie. "Shh, easy,

easy," she said, laying her cheek against his nose. "He's quieting down. He can't be hurt bad, don't you think? But where's all that blood coming from?" She leaned forward to touch the gelding's right shoulder, and the animal squealed and started struggling against the harness again.

"Leave it," Charley ordered, clamping a hand on her arm. "Wait for the vet. You could get hurt."

"Ne," she argued, but it wasn't a real protest. She didn't struggle against his grip. She knew he was right.

He nodded. "Just keep doing what you were." He held her arm a second longer than he needed to.

"Miriam!"

It was a woman's voice, one of her sisters', for sure. Charley released Miriam.

"Oh, Anna, come quick! Oh, it's terrible."

Charley glanced up. It was Miriam's twin, a big girl, more than a head taller and three times as wide. No one could ever accuse Anna of not being Plain. She wasn't ugly; she had nice eyes, but she couldn't hold a candle to Miriam. Still, he liked Anna well enough. She had a good heart and she baked the best biscuits in Kent County, maybe the whole state.

"Don't cry, Anna," Miriam said. "You'll set me to crying again."

"How bad are they hurt?" Miriam's older sister Ruth came to stand on the bank beside Anna. She was holding Miriam's filthy white *kapp.* "Are you all right? Is she all right?" She glanced from Miriam to Charley.

"I'm fine," Miriam assured her. "Just muddy. It's Molly and Blackie I'm worried about."

Fat tears rolled down Anna's broad cheeks. "I'm glad Susanna's not here," she said. "I made her stay in the kitchen. She shouldn't see this."

"Did Irwin go to call the vet?" Charley asked. "We told him—"

"Ya." Anna wiped her face with her apron. "He ran fast. Took the shortcut across the fields."

"Is there anything I can do?" Ruth called down. "Should I come—?"

"Ne," Miriam answered. "Watch for the vet. And send Irwin to the school to tell Mam as soon as he gets back." The mare groaned pitifully, and Miriam glanced over at her. "She'll be all right," she said. "God willing, she will be all right."

"I'll pray for them," Anna said. "That I can do." She caught the corner of her apron and balled it in a big hand. "For the horses."

Charley heard the dinner bell ringing from the Yoder farmhouse. "Maybe that's Irwin," he said to Miriam. "A good idea. We'll need help to get the horses up." The repeated sounding of the bell would signal the neighbors. Other Amish would come from the surrounding farms. There would be many strong hands to help with the animals, once it was considered safe to move them.

"There's the Hartmans' truck," Ruth said. She waved, and Charley heard the engine. "I hope he doesn't get stuck, trying to cross the field. The lane's awfully muddy."

Miriam looked at him, her eyes wide with hope. "It will be all right, won't it, Charley?"

"God willing," he said.

"It's John," Anna exclaimed. "He's getting out of the truck with his bag."

Great, Charley thought. It would have to be John and not his uncle Albert. He sighed. He supposed that John knew his trade. He'd saved the Beachys' Jersey cow when everyone had given it up for dead. But once the

Mennonite man got here, Miriam would have eyes only for John with his fancy education and his English clothes. Whenever John was around, he and Miriam put their heads together and talked like they were best friends.

"John must have been close by. Maybe it's a good sign." Miriam looked at him earnestly.

"Ya," he agreed, without much enthusiasm. He knew that it was uncharitable to put his own jealousy before the lives of her beloved horses. *"Ya,"* he repeated. "It's lucky he came so quick." *Lucky for Molly and Blackie,* he thought ruefully, *but maybe not for me.*

Chapter Two

He'd witnessed a true blessing today, Charley thought as he watched John bandaging Blackie's hind leg. Both animals had needed stitches and Molly had several deep cuts, but neither horse had suffered a broken bone. Between the sedative the young vet had administered and the help of neighbors, they'd been able to get the team back to the barn where they now stood in fresh straw in their stalls.

Charley had to admit that John knew what he was doing. He was ashamed of his earlier reluctance to have him come to the Yoder farm. With God's help, both animals would recover. Even the sight of Miriam standing so close to John, listening intently to his every word, didn't trouble Charley much. It was natural that Miriam would be worried about her horses and John was a very good vet. Reading anything more into it was his own insecurity. After all, John wasn't Amish; he didn't have a chance with Miriam. She would never choose a husband outside her faith.

Since she was a child, Miriam had had a gift for healing animals. When his Holstein calf had gotten tangled in a barbed wire fence, it had been ten-year-old Miriam who'd come every afternoon to rub salve on the calf's neck while he held it still. Later that year, she'd helped his mother deliver twin lambs in a snowstorm, and the following summer Miriam had set a broken leg on his brother's goat. More than one neighbor called on Miriam instead of the vet for trouble with their animals. Some men in the community seemed to forget she was a girl and asked her advice before they bought a cow or a driving horse.

If Miriam had been born English, Charley supposed that she might have gone to college to study veterinary medicine herself, but their people didn't believe in that much schooling. For the Old Order Amish, eighth grade was the end of formal education. He'd been glad to leave school at fourteen, but for Miriam, it had been a sacrifice. She had a hunger to know more about animal doctoring, so it was natural that she and John would find a lot to talk about.

"I think we can fix the hay wagon, but a good third of the hay is wet through."

"What?" Startled, Charley turned to see Eli standing beside him. He'd been so busy thinking about Miriam that he hadn't even heard Eli enter the barn.

"The hay wagon," Eli repeated. He glanced at John and Miriam and then cut his eyes at Charley, but he kept talking. "Front and back wheel on the one side need replacing, as well as some broken boards, but the axles are sound. We should be able to make it right in a few hours."

Eli was sharp and not just with crafting wood. Charley could tell that he hadn't missed the ease between Miriam and the Mennonite boy, or Charley's unease at their friendship.

"Right." Charley nodded. Eli was his friend and Ruth's

intended. Charley had been working on the foundation for their new house today. Otherwise, he wouldn't have been at the Yoder place and close enough to reach Miriam when the accident happened. *God's mysterious ways,* he thought, and then said to Eli, "Maybe we can get together some night after chores."

"Ya," Eli agreed with a twinkle in his eye. "No problem."

"I don't know what we would have done without you," Miriam said to John as he opened the stall door for her. "When the hay wagon overturned, I was so afraid…"

Charley could hear the emotion in her voice. It made him want to walk over to her and put his arms around her. It made him want to protect her from anything bad that could ever happen to her. Instead, he stood there, feeling like a bumpkin, listening in on her and John's conversation.

"You didn't panic. That's the most important thing with horses," John said, speaking way too gently to suit Charley. "It's a good thing you didn't try to get them up without help. It could have been a lot worse if I hadn't been able to sedate them."

I'm the one who told Miriam to wait, Charley wanted to remind them. *That was my decision.* But again, he didn't say what he was thinking. He knew he was being petty and that pettiness could eat a man up inside. How did the English refer to jealousy? A green-eyed monster?

Miriam looked over toward Charley, noticed him watching them and smiled, making his heart do a little flip. Why hadn't he ever noticed how sweet her smile was?

"You were there when I needed you, too," she said. "I was so scared. One of them could have been killed."

I was terrified, but for you more than the horses. It seemed like it took an hour for me to run across the field to see if you were hurt. The words caught in his throat. He couldn't spit them out, not in front of John and Eli. Usually, he had no trouble giving his opinion, flirting with girls, cracking jokes, being good-natured Charley, everybody's friend. But not today…today he was as tongue-tied as Irwin.

He couldn't tear his eyes away from Miriam. She was wearing a modest blue dress now, a properly starched *kapp* and a clean white apron. As soon as they'd gotten the horses out of the creek and headed back toward the barn, her sisters had rushed her to the house to put on dry clothes. The blue suited her. It was almost the color of a robin's egg, without the speckles. Her red hair was freshly-combed and braided, pinned up and mostly hidden under her *kapp,* but he couldn't help remembering how it had looked in the sunlight.

This morning, he'd been a bachelor, with no more thoughts of tying himself down in marriage any time soon than trying to fly off the barn roof. He'd certainly known that he'd have to get serious in a few years, and start a family, but not yet. He had years of running around to do yet—lots of girls to tease and frolics to enjoy. Now, in the time it took that wagon to overturn, his life had changed direction. After seeing Miriam this way today, he realized that what mattered most to him was winning her hand and having the right to watch her take her *kapp* off and brush out that red-gold hair every night.

Unconsciously, he tugged his wide-brimmed straw hat lower on his forehead, hoping no one would notice his embarrassment, but Miriam didn't miss a trick. She reached up and pressed her hand to his cheek. The touch of her palm sent a jolt through him, and he jumped back, heat flashing under his skin. He was certain it made him look even more the fool.

"Charley Byler, what's wrong with you?" she demanded. "You're red as a *banty* rooster. And your clothes are still soaked. Are you taking a chill? You'd best come up to the house, and drink some hot coffee."

"Can't." He backed off as if she were contagious. He couldn't take the chance she'd touch him again. Not here. Not in front of the Mennonite. "Got to pick up Mary," he said in a rush. "Thursdays. In Dover." Every Thursday, his sister cleaned house for an English woman and his mother depended on him to bring her home. "She'll be expecting me."

"I forgot," Miriam said. "That's too bad. Mam and Anna are cooking an early supper, since we all missed our noon meal. I think they've been cooking since Mam got home from school. She wanted me to invite you and John to join us for fried chicken and dumplings. You're welcome to bring Mary, too."

"Ne." He pushed his hat back. "Guess we'll get home to evening chores."

Shadows were lengthening in the big barn, but Miriam could read the disappointment on his face. She could tell he wanted to have dinner with them, so why didn't he just come back after he picked up his sister? She didn't know what was going on with Charley, but she could tell something was bothering him. She'd known him long enough to know that look on his face.

"Another time for certain," Charley said, and fled the barn.

"Ya," she called after him. "Another time."

"Well, since Charley can't come, maybe there's room for me at the table," Eli said.

She folded her arms, turning to him. "I didn't think I had to invite you. You're family. I bet Ruth's already set a plate for you." She smiled and he smiled back. Miriam was so happy for Ruth. Eli really did love her, and despite his rocky start in the community, he was going to make a good husband to her.

"Good," Eli said, "because I've worked up such an appetite pulling those horses out of the creek, that I can eat my share and Charley's, too."

Eli lived with his uncle Roman and aunt Fannie near the chair shop where he worked as a cabinetmaker, but since he and Ruth had declared their intentions, he ate in the Yoder kitchen more evenings than not.

Miriam looked back at John expectantly. "Supper?"

"I don't want to impose on your mother." John knelt beside a bale of straw and closed up his medical case. "Uncle Albert is picking up something at the deli for—"

"You may as well give in," Miriam interrupted. She rested one hand on her hip. "Mam won't let you off the farm until she's stuffed you like a Christmas turkey. We're all grateful you came so quickly."

John picked up the chest. "Then, I suppose I should stay. I wouldn't want to upset Hannah."

She chuckled, surprised he actually accepted her invitation, but pleased. She knew that he rarely got a home-cooked meal since he'd come to work with his grandfather and uncle in their veterinary practice. None of the three bachelors could cook. When he stopped by her stand at Spence's, the auction and bazaar where they sold produce and baked goods twice a week, he always looked longingly at the lunch she brought from home. Sometimes, she took pity on him and shared her potato salad, peach pie, or roast beef sandwiches.

Blackie thrust his head over the stall door and nudged her, hay falling from his mouth. Miriam stroked his neck. "You've had a rough day, haven't you, boy?" She took a sugar cube out of her apron pocket and fed it to him, savoring the warmth of his velvety lips against her hand. Then she walked back to check on Molly. The dapple-gray was standing, head down dejectedly, hind foot in the air, unwilling to put any weight on it. That was the hoof that she'd been treating for a stone bruise for the last week, and the thing that concerned John the most. He was afraid that the accident would now make the problem worse.

"Do you think I should stay with her tonight?" Miriam asked, fingering one of her *kapp* ribbons.

"Nothing more you can do now." John moved to her side and looked at Molly. "She needs time for that sedative to wear off and then I can get a better idea of how much pain she's in. I'll come back and check on her again before I leave and I'll stop by tomorrow. I need to see that the two of them are healing and I want to keep an eye on that hoof."

"Supper's ready!" Ruth pushed open the top of the Dutch door. "And bring your appetites. Mam and Anna have cooked enough food to feed half the church."

"Charley had to pick up his sister in Dover so he left," Miriam said, "but John and Eli have promised to eat double to make up for it."

"Charley can't eat with us?" Ruth pushed wide the bottom half of the barn door and stepped into the shadowy passageway. "That's a shame."

"*Ya,*" Miriam agreed. "A shame." Ruth liked Charley. So did Anna, Rebecca, Leah, Johanna, Susanna and especially Mam. The trouble was, ever since the school picnic last spring, when Charley had bought her pie and they'd shared a box lunch, her sisters and Mam acted like they expected the two of them to be a couple. All the girls at church thought the two of them were secretly courting.

"Lucky for you that Charley was nearby when the wagon turned over," Eli said. He and Ruth exchanged looks. "He's a good man, Charley."

Miriam glared at Ruth, who assumed an innocent expression. "It's John you should thank," Miriam said. "Without him, we might have lost both Molly and Blackie."

"But Charley pulled you out of the creek." Ruth followed Eli out into the barnyard. "He might have saved your life."

Miriam could barely keep from laughing. "Charley's the one who nearly drowned me. And the water isn't deep enough to drown a goose." She glanced back at John. "Pay no attention to either of them. Since they decided to get married, they've become matchmakers."

"So, you and Charley?" John asked. "Are you—?"

"*Ne!*" she declared. "He's like a brother to me. We're friends, nothing more." It was true. They *were* friends, nothing more and no amount of nudging by her family could make her feel differently. When the right man came along, she'd know it…*if* the right man came along. Otherwise, she was content staying here on the farm, doing the work she loved best and helping her mother and younger sisters.

Ruth led the way up onto the back porch where Miriam and the two men stopped at the outdoor sink to wash their hands. John looked at the large pump bottle of antibacterial soap and raised one eyebrow quizzically.

Miriam chuckled. "What did you expect? Lye soap?"

"No." He grinned at her. "People just think that…"

"Amish live like George Washington," she finished. Ruth and Eli were having a tug of war with the towel, but she ignored their silly game and met John's gaze straight on. "We don't," she said. "We use all sorts of modern conveniences—indoor bathrooms, motor-driven washing machines, telephones." She smiled mischievously. "We even have young, know-it-all Mennonite veterinarians."

"Ouch." He grabbed his middle and pretended to be in pain. Then, he shrugged. "Lots of people have strange ideas about my faith, too. My sister gets mistaken for being Amish all the time."

"Because of her *kapp*," Miriam agreed. "Tell her that I had an English woman at Spence's last week ask me if I was Mennonite."

"I'll admit, I didn't know much about you until I came here. I was surprised that the practice had so many Amish clients." Eli tossed the towel to him and he offered it to her.

"Of course. We have a lot of animals." She dried her hands and took a fresh towel off the shelf for him.

She liked John. He had a nice smile. He was a nice-looking young man. Nice, dark brown hair, cropped short in a no-nonsense cut, a straight nose and a good strong chin. Maybe not as pretty in the face as Eli, who was the most handsome man she'd ever seen, but almost as tall.

John was slim, rather than compact like Charley, with the faintest shadow of a dark beard on his cheeks. His fingers were long and slender; his nails clean and trimmed short. When he walked or moved his hands or arms, as he did when he hung the damp towel on the hook, he did it gracefully. John seemed like a gentle man with a quiet air of confidence and strength. It was one of the reasons she believed that he was so good with livestock and maybe why he made her feel so at ease when they were together.

"Miriam, John, come to the table," Mam called through the screen door. "The food is hot."

It wasn't until then that Miriam noticed that Ruth and Eli had gone inside, while she and John had stood there woolgathering and staring at each other. Would he think her slow-witted, that it took her so long to wash the barn off her hands?

"*Ya,* we're coming," she answered. She pushed open the door for John, but he stopped and motioned for her to go through first. He was English in so many ways, yet not. John was an interesting person and she was glad he'd accepted Mam's invitation to eat with them.

Her sisters, Irwin and Eli were already seated. Mam waved John to the chair at the head of the table, reserved for guests, since her father's death. She took her own place between Ruth and her twin, Anna. Since John knew everyone but Anna and Susanna, she introduced them before everyone bowed their heads to say grace in silence.

Miriam hadn't thought she was hungry, but just the smell of the food made her ravenous. Besides the chicken and dumplings, Mam and Anna had made broccoli, coleslaw, green beans and yeast bread. There were pickled beets, mashed potatoes and homemade applesauce. She glanced at John and noticed that his gaze was riveted on the big crockery bowl of slippery dumplings.

Mam asked Irwin to pass the chicken to John and the big kitchen echoed with the sound of clinking forks, the clatter of dishes and easy conversation. Susanna, youngest and most outspoken of her sisters, made Mam and Eli laugh when she screwed up her little round face and demanded to know where John's hat was.

"My hat?" he asked.

"When you came in, you didn't put your hat on the coatrack. Eli and Irwin put their hats on the coatrack. Where's yours?"

Miriam was about to signal Susanna to hush, thinking she would explain later to her that unlike the Amish, Mennonite men didn't have to wear hats. But then Irwin piped up. "Maybe Molly ate it."

"Or Jeremiah," Eli suggested, pointing to Irwin's little dog, stretched out beside the woodstove.

"Or Blackie," Anna said.

"Maybe he lost it in the creek," Ruth teased.

John smiled at Susanna. "Nope," he said. "I think a frog stole it when we were pulling the horses out."

"Oh," Susanna replied, wide-eyed.

John was teasing Susanna, but it was easy for Miriam to see that he wasn't poking fun *at* her. He was treating her just as he would Anna or Ruth, if he knew them better. Sometimes, because Susanna had been born with Down syndrome, people didn't know how to act around her. She was a little slow to grasp ideas or tackle new tasks, but no one had a bigger heart. It made Miriam feel good inside to see John fitting in so well at their table, almost as if the family had known him for years.

"We won't forget what you did for the horses," Mam said. "Even if they did eat your hat."

Everyone laughed at that and Susanna laughed the loudest. It was the best ending to a terrible day that Miriam could ask for, and by the time John had finished his second slice of apple pie, she was sure that he had enjoyed his meal with them as much as they'd enjoyed his company.

Later, after she and John and Ruth and Eli had inspected the horses, John drove away in his pickup. He had one final house call before calling it a day. Eli left as well, wanting to clean the chair shop for his uncle. That left Miriam and Ruth to do the milking. Irwin drove the cows in and offered to help, but Miriam sent him off to see if Mam needed anything. Irwin was shaping up to be a good gardener, but he didn't know the first thing about milking and usually ended up getting kicked by a cow or spilling a bucket of milk.

Miriam looked forward to this time of day. She and Ruth had always been close friends and soon Ruth would be in her own home with her own cow to milk. Miriam would miss her. She loved her twin Anna dearly; she loved all her sisters, but Ruth was the kind of big sister she could talk to about anything. Of course there were some nights when Miriam might have preferred to milk alone.

"You know he's sweet on you," Ruth said. She was milking a black-and-white Holstein cow named Bossy in the next stall. Ruth had her head pushed into Bossy's sagging middle and two streams of milk hissed into her bucket in a steady rhythm.

"Who likes me?" Miriam stopped a few feet from Bossy's tail, her empty bucket in one hand and a three-legged milking stool in the other. She'd tied a scarf over her *kapp* to keep it clean and pushed back her sleeves.

"Charley. He's going to make someone a fine husband."

"I know he is. It's just not going to be me." Miriam sighed and walked to the next stall where Polly, a brown Jersey, waited patiently, chewing her cud. "And I'm tired of you and Anna trying to make something of it that isn't."

"You like the cute vet better?"

Polly swished her tail and Miriam pushed it out of the

way as she placed her stool on the cement floor and sat down. "John?"

"Was there another cute vet at supper?"

"He came because we needed him. It's his job."

"*Ya,* but you like him." Ruth's voice was muffled by the cow's belly. "Admit it."

Miriam took a soapy cloth and carefully washed Polly's bag. The cow swished her tail again. Miriam dropped the cloth into the washbasin and took hold of one teat. She squeezed and pulled gently and milk squirted into the bucket. "First Charley, then John."

"He's Mennonite," Ruth said.

"I know he's Mennonite."

"But you think he's cute."

Miriam wished her sister was standing close enough to squirt with a spray of milk. Once Ruth started, there was no stopping her. "Mam invited him to dinner, not me."

"But you like him. Better than Charley."

"Maybe I do and maybe I don't," she said. "But if you say another word about boys tonight, I'll dump this bucket of milk over your head."

It was dusk by the time John got back to the house that was both office and home for him, his grandfather and Uncle Albert. John completed his paperwork, refilled his portable medicine chest and went upstairs to shower. Once he'd changed into clean clothing, he wandered out onto the side porch where the two older men sat with their feet propped up on the rail, sipping tall glasses of lemonade. As always, the three shared the day's incidents. When his grandfather asked, John began telling them about the accident at the Yoder farm.

The third time John mentioned Miriam's name, his

uncle Albert asked him if he was sweet on her. John shrugged and took a big sip of lemonade.

"She's Old Order Amish," his grandfather said.

"I know that," John replied.

"Miriam, is she one of the twins?" his uncle asked.

"I think so."

"The big one or the little one?"

"The little one."

"Pretty as a picture," Uncle Albert observed.

"Yeah," John admitted, getting up and attempting a quick escape into the house before they pressed the issue any further.

Truth be told, he *was* sweet on Miriam Yoder and he was pretty certain she liked him. And it wasn't just her looks or the physical chemistry between them that attracted him. She was easy to talk to and shared his love of animals. Although he always knew he would marry and have children someday, John hadn't seriously dated since his final year of vet school, when his girlfriend of three years had broken up with him. Alyssa, the daughter of a Baptist minister, had broken his heart and after that he had filled in what little spare time he had with family. It had been so long that he had forgotten what it felt like to be so strongly attracted to a woman. The fact that Miriam was Amish complicated the matter even further.

His grandfather chuckled. "He's sweet on her."

"Good luck with that," Uncle Albert said. "I've heard those Yoder girls can be a handful."

John paused in the doorway and looked back. "Sometimes," he said softly, "a handful is just the kind of woman a man is looking for."

Chapter Three

Miriam and Anna were just setting the table for breakfast the following morning when they heard the sound of a wagon rumbling up their lane. Miriam, who'd showered after morning chores, snatched a kerchief off the peg and covered her damp hair before going to the kitchen door. "It's Charley," she called back as she walked out onto the porch. He reined in his father's team at the hitching rail near the back steps.

"Morning." The wagon was piled high with bales of hay.

"You're up and about early," she said, tucking as much of her hair out of sight as possible. Wet strands tumbled down her back, and she gave up trying to hide them. After all, it was only Charley.

"Where are you off to?" Behind her, Jeremiah yipped and hopped up and down with excitement. "Hush, hush," she said to the dog. "Irwin! Call him. He'll frighten Charley's team."

Irwin opened the screen door and scooped up the little animal. "Morning, Charley," he said.

Charley climbed down from the wagon. "I'm coming

here," he said as he tied the horses to the hitching rail. "Here." .

"What?" she asked. Curious, Irwin followed her down the porch steps into the yard, the whining dog in his arms.

Charley laughed. "You wanted to know where I was going, didn't you?"

She wrinkled her nose. "I don't understand. We didn't buy any hay from your father."

"Ne." He grinned at her. "But you lost a lot of your load in the creek. My Dat and Samuel and your uncle Reuben wanted to help."

She sighed. The hay she'd lost had already been paid for. There was no extra money to buy more. "It's good of you," she said, "but our checking account—"

"This is a gift to help replace what you lost."

"All that?" Irwin asked. "That's a lot."

She looked at the wagon, mentally calculating the number of bales stacked on it. "We didn't have that much to begin with," she said, "and not all our bales were ruined."

Charley tilted his straw hat with an index finger and chuckled. "Don't be so pigheaded, Miriam. I'm putting this in your barn. You'll take it with grace, or explain to your uncle Reuben, the preacher, why you cannot accept a gift from the members of your church who love you."

Moisture stung the back of her eyelids, and a lump rose in her throat. *"Ya,"* she managed. "It is kind of you all."

Charley had always been kind. Since she'd been a child, she'd known that she could always count on him in times of trouble. When her father had died, without being asked Charley had taken over the chores and organized the young men to set up tables for supper after the funeral and carry messages to everyone in the neighbor-hood. A good man…a pleasant-looking man—even if he did usually need a haircut. *But he's just not the man I'd want for a husband,* she thought, recalling her conver-sation with Ruth last night. *Not for me, no matter what everyone else thinks.*

He walked toward her, solid, sandy-haired Charley, bits of hay clinging to his pants and shirt, and pale blue eyes dancing. *Pure joy of God's good life,* her father called that sparkle in some folks' eyes. He was such a *nice* guy, perfect for a friend. Ruth was right, he would make someone a good husband; he would be perfect for sweet Anna. But Charley was a *catch* and he'd pick a cute little bride with a bit of land and a houseful of brothers, not her dear Plain sister.

"We're family. We look out for our neighbors."

She nodded, so full of gratitude that she wanted to hug him. This is what the English never saw, how they lived with an extended family that would never see one of their own do without.

"I'm happy to make the delivery and I'd not turn down a cup of coffee," Charley said. "Or a sausage biscuit, if it was offered." He gestured toward the house. "That's Anna's homemade sausage I smell, isn't it? She seasons it better than the butcher shop."

"Ya," Irwin said. "It's Anna's sausage, fresh ground. And pancakes and eggs."

Miriam laughed. "We're just sitting down to breakfast. Would you like to join us?"

"Are Reuben's sermons long?" Charley chuckled at his own jest as he brushed hay from his pants. "I missed last night's supper. I'm not going to turn down a second chance at Anna's cooking." Then he glanced back toward the barn. "How are your horses?"

"Blackie's stiff, but his appetite is fine. Molly's no worse. I got her to eat a little grain this morning, but she's still favoring that hoof. John said he'd stop by this afternoon." She followed him up onto the porch and into the house. Irwin and the dog trailed after them.

"Miriam invited me to breakfast," Charley announced as he entered the kitchen, leaving his straw hat on a peg near the door.

Mam rose from her place. "It's good to have you."

"He brought us a load of hay," Miriam explained, grabbing a plate and extra silverware before sitting down. She set the place setting beside hers and scooted over on the bench to make room for him. "A gift from Uncle Reuben, Samuel and Charley's father."

Ruth smiled at him as she passed a plate of buckwheat pancakes to their guest. "It's good of you. Of all who thought of us."

"I mean to spread those bales that got wet," Charley explained, needing no further invitation to heap his plate high with pancakes. "If the rain holds off, it could dry out again. I wouldn't give it to the horses, but for the cows—"

"We could rake it up and pile it loose in the barn when it dries," Miriam said, thinking out loud. "That could work. It's a good idea."

"A good idea," Susanna echoed.

The clock on the mantel chimed the half hour. "Ach, I'll be late for school," Mam exclaimed. She took another swallow of coffee and got to her feet. When Charley started to rise, she waved him back. "*Ne,* you eat your fill. It's my fault I'm running late. The girls and I were chattering like wrens this morning and I didn't watch the time. Come, Irwin. There will be no excuses of illness today."

Irwin popped up, rolling his last bit of sausage into a pancake and taking it with him.

"It wouldn't do for the teacher to be late." Anna collected Mam's and Irwin's dinner buckets and handed them out. "Have a good day."

"Good day," Irwin mumbled through a mouthful of sausage and pancake as he dodged out the door. "Watch Jeremiah, Susanna!"

"I will," she called after him, obviously proud to be given such an important job every day. "He's a good dog for me," she announced to no one in particular.

"Don't forget to meet me at the school after dinner with the buggy." Mam tied her black bonnet under her chin. "Since there's only a half day today, we've plenty of time to drive to Johnson's orchard."

"I won't," Miriam answered. Their neighbor, Samuel Mast, who was sweet on Mam, had loaned them a driving horse until Blackie recovered from his injuries. They'd have apples ripe in a few weeks here on the farm, but Mam liked to get an early start on her applesauce and canned apples. The orchard down the road had several early varieties that made great applesauce.

Once their mother was out the door, they continued the hearty meal. Miriam had been up since five and she suspected that Charley had been, too. They were all hungry and it would be hours until dinner. Having him at the table was comfortable; he was like family. Everyone liked him, even Irwin, who was rarely at ease with anyone other than her Mam and her sisters.

The only sticky moments of the pleasant breakfast were when Charley began to ask questions about John. "You say he's coming back today?"

Miriam nodded. "The stitches need to stay in for a few days, but John wants to have a look at them today."

"He thinks he has to look at 'em himself? You tell him you could do it? I know something about stitches. We both do."

"He *likes* Miriam," Susanna supplied, smiling and nodding. "He always comes and talks, talks, talks to her at the sale. And sometimes he buys her a soda—orange, the kind she likes. Ruffie says that Miriam had better watch out, because Mennonite boys are—"

"Hard workers," Ruth put in.

Susanna's eyes widened. "But that's not what you said," she insisted. "You said—"

Anna tipped over her glass, spilling water on Susanna's skirt.

Susanna squealed and jumped up. "Oops." She giggled. "You made a mess, Anna."

"I did, didn't I?" Anna hurried to get a dishtowel to mop up the water on the tablecloth.

"My apron is all wet," Susanna announced.

"It's fine," Miriam soothed. "Eat your breakfast." She rose to bring the coffeepot to the table and pour Charley another cup. "I heard your father had a tooth pulled last week," she said, changing the conversation to a safer subject.

After they had eaten, Miriam offered to help Charley unload the hay, but he suggested she finish cleaning up breakfast dishes with her sisters. A load of hay was nothing to him, he said as he went out the door, giving Susanna a wink.

"What did I tell you?" Ruth said when the girls were alone in the kitchen. "People are beginning to talk about you and John Hartman, seeing you at the sale together every week. He's definitely sweet on you, even Charley noticed."

"I don't see him at Spence's *every week*," Miriam argued.

Ruth lifted an eyebrow.

"So he likes to stop for lunch there on Fridays," Miriam said.

"And visit with you," Ruth said. "I'm telling you, he likes you and it's plain enough that Charley saw it."

"That's just Charley. You know how he is." Miriam gestured with her hand. "He's…protective of us."

"Of you," Anna said softly.

"Of all of us," Miriam insisted. "I haven't done anything wrong and neither has John, so enough about it already." She went into the bathroom and quickly braided her hair, pinned it up and covered it with a clean *kapp*.

When she came back into the kitchen, Anna was washing dishes and Susanna was drying them. Ruth was grating cabbage for the noon meal. "I've got outside chores to do so I'm going to go on out if you don't need me in here," Miriam said.

Ruth concentrated on the growing pile of shredded cabbage.

Miriam wasn't fooled. "What? Why do you have that look on your face? You don't believe me? John is a friend, nothing more. Can't I have a friend?"

"Of course you can," Ruth replied. "Just don't do anything to worry Mam. She has enough on her mind. Johanna—" She stopped, as if having second thoughts about what she was going to say.

"What about Johanna?" Miriam didn't think her sister Johanna had been herself lately. Johanna lived down the road with her husband and two small children, but sometimes they didn't see her for a week at a time and that concerned Miriam. When she was first married, Johanna had been up to the house almost every day. Miriam knew her sister had more responsibilities since the babies had come along, but she sometimes got the impression Johanna was hiding something. "Are Jonah and the baby well?"

"Everyone is fine," Anna said.

"Later," Ruth promised, glancing meaningfully at Susanna. "I'll tell you all I know, later."

"I'll hold you to it," Miriam said. She thought about Johanna while she fed and watered the laying hens and the pigs. If no one was sick, what could the problem be? And why hadn't Mam said anything to her about it? Once she'd finished up with the animals, she went to the barn to give Charley a hand.

Dat had rigged a tackle to a crossbeam and they used the system of ropes and pulleys to hoist the heavy hay bales up into the loft. It was hard work, but with two of them, it went quick enough. They talked about all sorts of things, nothing important, just what was going on in their lives: Ruth and Eli's wedding, harvesting crops, the next youth gathering.

After sending the last bale up, Miriam walked to the foot of the loft ladder. Charley stood above her, hat off, wiping the sweat off his forehead with a handkerchief. "I'm coming up," she said.

He moved back and offered his hand when she reached the top rung. She took it, climbed up into the shadowy loft and looked around at the neat stacks of hay. It smelled heavenly. It was quiet here, the only sounds the cooing of pigeons and Charley's breathing. Charley squeezed her fingers in his and she suddenly realized he was still holding her hand, or she was holding his; she wasn't quite sure which it was.

She quickly tucked her hand behind her back and

averted her gaze, as a small thrill of excitement passed through her.

"Miriam," he began.

She backed toward the ladder. "I just wanted to see the hay," she stammered, feeling all off-kilter. She didn't know why but she felt like she needed to get away from Charley, like she needed to catch her breath. "I've got things to do."

"What you two doin' up there?" Susanna called up the ladder. "Can I come up?"

"*Ne!* I'm coming down," Miriam answered, descending the ladder so fast that her hands barely touched the rungs.

Charley followed her. He jumped off the ladder when he was three feet off the ground and landed beside her with a solid *thunk*.

"I came to see how Molly is." Susanna looked at Miriam and then at Charley. "Something wrong?"

Miriam felt her cheeks grow warm. *"Ne."* She brushed hay from her apron, feeling completely flustered and not knowing why. She'd held Charley's hand plenty of times before. What made this time different? She could still feel the strength of his grip and wondered if this feeling of bubbly warmth that reached from her belly to the tips of her toes was temptation. No wonder handholding by unmarried couples was frowned upon by the elders.

"Ne," Charley repeated. "Nothing wrong." But he was looking at Miriam strangely.

Something had changed between them in those few seconds up in the hayloft and Miriam wasn't sure what. She could hear it in Charley's voice. She could feel it in her chest, the way her heart was beating a little faster than it should be.

Susanna was still watching her carefully. "Anna said

to tell you to cut greens if you go in the garden and not
to forget to meet Mam."

The three stood there, looking at each other.

"Guess I should be going," Charley finally said, awk-
wardly looking down at his feet.

"Thanks again for bringing the hay, Charley. I can
always count on you." Miriam dared a quick look into
his eyes. "You're like the brother I never had."

"That's me. Good old Charley." He sounded upset with
her and she had no idea why.

"Don't be silly." She tapped his shoulder playfully.
"You're a lifesaver. You kept me from drowning in the
creek, didn't you?"

"In the creek? Right, like *you* needed saving." He
laughed, and she laughed with him, easing the tension
of the moment.

They walked out of the barn, side by side with Susanna trailing after them, and crossed the yard to the
well. Charley drew up a bucket of water, and all three
drank deeply from the dipper. Then he went back to the
barn to guide the team and wagon down the passageway
and out the far doors. By the time he'd turned his horses
around and driven out of the yard, Miriam had almost
stopped feeling as though she'd somehow let him down.
Almost...

Later, in the buggy on the way to the orchard with her
mother, Miriam had wanted to tell her about the strange
moment in the hayloft with Charley. In a large family,
even a loving one, time alone with parents was special.
Miriam was a grown woman, but Mam had a way of listening without judging and giving sound advice without
seeming to. Miriam valued her mother's opinion more
than anyone's, even more than Ruth's and the two of them

were the closest among the sisters. But this afternoon, she didn't want sisterly advice; she didn't need any more of Ruth's teasing about her friendship with John Hartman. Today, she needed her mother.

But before she could bring up Charley, she needed to find out what Ruth and Anna had been hinting about after breakfast, concerning Johanna. If Johanna had trouble, it certainly took priority over a silly little touch of a boy's hand. She was just about to ask about her older sister when Mam gestured for her to pull over into the Amish graveyard and rein in the horse.

Sometimes, Mam came here to visit Dat's grave, even though it wasn't something that their faith encouraged. The graves were all neat and well cared for; that went without saying, but no one believed their loved ones were here. Those that had died in God's grace abided with Him in heaven. Instead of mourning those who had lived out their earthly time, those left behind should be happy for them. But Mam—who'd been born and raised Mennonite—had her quirks and one of them was that she came here sometimes to talk to their father.

When Mam came to Dat's grave, she usually came alone. This was different and Miriam gave her mother her full attention.

"You know we had a letter from Leah on Monday," Mam said.

Miriam nodded. Her two younger sisters, Leah and Rebecca, had been in Ohio for over six months caring for their father's mother and her sister, Aunt Jezebel. *Grossmama* had broken a hip falling down her cellar stairs a year ago, and although the bone had healed, her general health seemed to be getting worse. Aunt Ida, Dat's sister, and her husband lived on the farm next to *Grossmama,* but her own constitution wasn't the best, and she'd asked

Mam for the loan of one of her girls. Mam had sent two, because neither *Grossmama* nor Aunt Jezebel, at their ages, could be expected to act as a proper chaperone for a young, unbaptized woman. No one, least of all Miriam, had expected the sisters to be away so long.

"What I didn't tell you," Mam continued, "was that this arrived on Tuesday from Rebecca." She removed an envelope from her apron pocket. "You'd best read it yourself."

Miriam slipped three lined sheets of paper out of the envelope and unfolded them. Rebecca's handwriting was neat and bold. Her sister had wanted to follow their mother's example and teach school. She'd gotten special permission from the bishop to continue her education by mail, but in spite of her sterling grades, no teaching positions in Amish schools had opened in Kent County.

Miriam skimmed over the opening and inquiries over Mam's health to see what Mam was talking about. It wasn't like her to keep secrets, and the fact that she hadn't said anything about what was in the letter was out of the ordinary and disturbing.

As she read through the pages, Miriam quickly saw how serious the problem was. According to Rebecca, their grandmother had moved beyond forgetfulness and both sisters were concerned for her safety. *Grossmama* had never been an easy person to please, and Leah and Rebecca had been chosen to go because they were the best-suited to the job.

Dat had been their grandmother's only son and she'd never approved of his choice of a bride. She'd made it clear from the beginning that she didn't like Mam. Even as the years passed, she never missed an opportunity to find fault with her and her daughters. Miriam had always tried to remember her duty to her grandmother and to remain charitable when discussing her with her sisters, but the truth was, the prospect of *Grossmama*'s extended visit for Ruth's marriage was something Miriam wasn't looking forward to.

According to Rebecca's letter, *Grossmama* had accidentally started fires in the kitchen twice. She'd taken to rising from her bed in the wee hours and wandering outside in her nightclothes, and was having unexplained bouts of temper, throwing objects at Leah and Rebecca and even at Aunt Jezebel. *Grossmama* had also begun to tell untruths about them to the neighbors. She refused to take her prescriptions because she was convinced that Aunt Jezebel was trying to poison her.

Miriam finished the letter and dropped it into her lap. "This is terrible," she said. "What can we do?"

Mam's eyes glistened with unshed tears. "I've been praying for an answer."

Miriam closed her hand over her mother's. "But why didn't you tell us?"

"I've talked to your aunt Martha."

"Aunt Martha?" If anyone could make a situation worse, it would be Dat's sister. "And…"

"She is *Grossmama*'s daughter. I'm only a daughter-in-law," Mam reminded her. "Anyway, Martha thinks that Rebecca may be exaggerating. She thinks we should go on as we are until they come here for the wedding."

"While *Grossmama* burns down the house around my sisters?"

Mam laughed. "I hope it's not that bad. As Rebecca says, she and Leah take turns keeping watch over her and they turn off the gas to the stove at night."

"But why isn't Aunt Martha or Aunt Ida or one of the other aunts doing something? She's *their* mother!"

"And she was Jonas's mother, my mother-in-law. God

has blessed us, child. We're better off financially than either of your aunts. Martha's house is small and she's already caring for Uncle Reuben's cousin Roy. If your father was alive, he'd feel it was his duty to care for his mother. We can't neglect that responsibility because he isn't here, can we?"

"You mean *Grossmama* is coming to live with us?" Miriam couldn't imagine such a thing. Her grandmother would destroy their peaceful home. She was demanding and so strict, she didn't even want to see children playing on church Sundays. She objected to youth singings and frolics, and most of all, she couldn't abide animals in the house. She would forbid Irwin to let Jeremiah through the kitchen door.

"Nothing is decided," Mam said. "I spoke to Johanna on Tuesday evening. I meant to discuss it with the rest of you, but then you had the accident with the hay wagon and the time wasn't right. I just wanted time alone to tell you about this."

"Ruth doesn't know?"

"We'll share the letter with her when the time is right. She's so excited about her wedding plans and the new house, I don't want to spoil this special time for her. And Anna, well, you know how Anna is."

"She'd look for the best in it," Miriam conceded. "And she'd probably want to take a van out to Ohio tomorrow and make everything right for everyone."

Her mother nodded. "You're sensible, Miriam. And you have a good heart."

"What do you need me to do, Mam?"

"For now? Pray. Think on this and look into your heart. If what Rebecca says is true, we may have to open our home to your grandmother. If we do, it must be all of us, with no hanging back. We have to do this together."

"All right," Miriam promised. Thoughts of Charley and the uncomfortable moment with him faded to the back of her mind. Her family—her mother—needed her. "But what shall we do right now?" she asked.

"Drive the horse to the orchard," Mam said with a smile. "We'll need those apples all the more with the wedding coming. We've got a lot of applesauce to make."

"*Grossmama* hates cinnamon in her applesauce."

"Does she?" Mam's eyes twinkled with mischief. "And I was just thinking we should stop at Byler's store to buy extra."

Chapter Four

Early Saturday morning, two days after Miriam's accident with the hay wagon, preparations began for Sunday church at Samuel Mast's home. Anna, Ruth, Mam and Susanna joined Miriam and most of the other women of their congregation to make Samuel's house ready for services and the communal meal that followed.

Since Samuel, the Yoders' closest neighbor, was a widower, he had no wife to supervise the food preparation and cleaning. Neighbors and members of the community always came to assist the host before a church day and Samuel was never at a lack for help. It seemed to Miriam as if every eligible Amish woman in the county, or a woman with a daughter or sister of marrying age, turned out to bake, cook, scrub and sweep until Samuel's rambling Victorian farmhouse shone like a new penny.

Miriam carried a bowl of potato salad in her right hand and one of coleslaw in her left as she crossed Samuel's spacious kitchen to a stone-lined pantry beyond. Although the September day was warm, huge blocks of ice in soapstone sinks kept the windowless room cool enough to keep food fresh for the weekend. A large kerosene-driven refrigerator along one wall held a sliced turkey

and two sliced hams, as well as a large tray of barbe-
cued chicken legs. Pies and cakes, pickles, chowchows
and jars of home-canned peaches weighed down shelves.
The widower might not have been a great cook, but he
never lacked for delicious food when it came to hosting
church.

As Miriam exited the pantry, closing the heavy door
carefully behind her, she nearly tripped over Anna, who
was down on her hands and knees scrubbing the kitchen
linoleum. At the sink, Ruth washed dishes and Johanna
dried and put them away while Mam arranged a bouquet
of autumn flowers on the oak table. "What can I do to
help?" Miriam asked.

Anna dug another rag out of the scrub bucket, wrung
it out and tossed it to her. Miriam caught the wet rag,
frowning with exaggeration at her sister.

"You asked." Anna grinned. She knew very well that
Miriam's strong point wasn't housework, but she also
knew that when it came down to it, her sister was a hard
worker, no matter what the task.

Chuckling, Miriam got down to assist Anna in finishing the floor. Johanna, who had a good voice, began
a hymn in High German, and Miriam, Anna and Ruth
joined in. Miriam's spirits lifted. Work always went faster
with many hands and a light heart, and the words to the
old song seemed to strike a chord deep inside her. It
was strange how scrubbing dirty linoleum could make a
person feel a part of God's great plan.

Aunt Martha had taken over the downstairs living
room and adjoining parlor, loudly directing her daughter Dorcas and several other young women in washing
windows, polishing the wood floors and arranging chairs.
But it didn't take long for Johanna's singing to spread
through the house. Soon, Dorcas's off-key soprano and

Aunt Martha's raspy tenor blended with the Yoder girls to make the walls ring with the joyful song of praise.

Samuel's sister, Louise Stutzman, came down the steep kitchen staircase, leading Samuel's daughter Mae, just as Johanna finished the chorus of their third hymn. The four-year-old was cranky, but Susanna, who'd come in the back door to find cookies, held out her arms and offered to take the little girl outside to play with the other small children.

"Gladly," Louise said, ushering Mae in Susanna's direction.

Susanna's round face beamed beneath her white *kapp*. "Don't worry. I'll take good care of her."

"I know you will, Susanna. All the children love you."

Susanna nodded. "You can bring baby Mae to our library. Mam says I am the best li-barian there is."

"Librarian," Mam corrected gently.

Susanna took a breath, grinned and repeated the word correctly. "Li-brarian!"

"Mam had our old milk house made into a lending library for the neighborhood," Anna explained. "Susanna helps people find books to take home. And she goes with Miriam to buy new ones that the children will like."

Louise smiled at Susanna. "That sounds like an important job."

"It is!" Susanna proclaimed. "You come and see. I'll find you a good book." Anna held the door open and Susanna carried a now-giggling Mae outside.

"Susanna has such a sweet spirit," Louise said. "You've been blessed, Hannah."

"I know," Mam agreed. "She's very special to us."

Miriam liked Samuel's older sister. She was a jolly person with a big smile and a good heart. She was always patient and kind to Susanna, never assuming that because of her Down syndrome, Susanna was less than safe to be trusted with Mae.

Louise had come from Ohio on Friday and brought Mae along for a visit with her father. When Samuel's wife died after a long illness, baby Mae was only a few months old. None of Samuel's family thought that he could manage an infant, since he already had the twins, Peter and Rudy, Naomi and Lori Ann to care for. Reluctantly, Samuel had agreed to let his sisters keep the baby temporarily, with the understanding that when he remarried, Mae would rejoin the family. Louise had offered to take Lori Ann as well, but Samuel wouldn't part with her.

Everyone thought that Samuel would marry after his year of mourning was up. And considering that he was the father of five, no one would have objected if he'd taken a new wife sooner. But it had been four years since Frieda had passed on, and Samuel seemed no closer to bringing a new bride home than he'd been on the day he'd ridden in the funeral procession to the graveyard.

Samuel made visits to his family in Ohio to see little Mae, and his mother and sisters brought the child to Delaware whenever it was his turn to host church services. The shared time was never very satisfactory for father or daughter. Mae was a difficult child, and Samuel and her sisters and brothers were strangers to her. The neighborhood agreed that the sooner Samuel took a wife and brought his family back together, the better for all.

The problem, as Miriam saw it, was that Samuel hadn't shown any real interest in any of the marriageable young women in the county or those his sisters paraded before him in Ohio. Samuel Mast was a catch. He was a devout member of the church, had a prosperous farm

and a pleasant disposition. And, he was a nice-looking
man, strong and healthy and full of fun. No one could
understand why he'd waited so long to remarry.

Miriam and the Yoder girls thought they knew why,
though.

Despite the difference in their ages—Samuel was eight
years younger than Mam—it looked to Miriam and her
sisters as if Samuel liked their mother. She and Ruth had
discussed the issue many times, usually late at night,
when they were in bed. They both thought Samuel was
a wonderful neighbor and a good man, but not the right
husband for Mam.

Hannah had been widowed two years and, by custom,
she should have remarried. The trouble was, she wasn't
ready, and neither were her daughters. Dat had been
special and Miriam couldn't see another man, not even
Samuel, sitting at the head of the table and taking charge
of their lives. Not yet at least.

Among the Plain people, a wife was supposed to
render obedience to her husband. Not that she didn't have
a strong role in the family or in the household; she did.
But a woman had to be subservient first to God, and then,
to her husband. Miriam couldn't imagine Mam being
subservient to anyone.

Growing up, Miriam had never heard her parents
argue. It seemed that Mam had always agreed with every
decision Dat ever made, but as Miriam grew older she
realized that, in reality, it was often Dat who'd listened
to Mam's advice, especially where their children were
concerned. In that way, Mam was different.

Mam had been born a Mennonite and had been baptized into the Amish church before they were married.
Miriam sometimes wondered if that was what made
her mother so strong-willed and independent. Would

another man, even a man as good-natured and as sweet as Samuel, be able to accept Mam's free spirit? Certainly, he'd ask her to give up teaching school. Married women didn't work outside the home.

If they married, would Samuel expect Mam to move into his house? What would happen to Dat's farm? To the Yoder girls, including herself? And what about Irwin? His closest relatives were Norman and Lydia Beachy; he'd lived with them when he first came to Seven Poplars, but that hadn't worked out well. That was why Irwin now lived with Miriam's family. If Mam and Samuel were to marry, would Samuel want to send Irwin back to the Beachy farm?

Mam and Miriam and her sisters had made out fine in the two years since Dat's death. It hadn't been easy, but they managed. There were a lot of ways a stepfather could disrupt the Yoder household, and thinking about it made Miriam uneasy. Ruth leaving to marry Eli was enough change for one year. Wasn't it?

"Whoa," Anna said. "That section of the floor is already done."

Miriam looked up. As usual, she'd been so deep in her thoughts that she'd forgotten to pay attention to what she was doing. "Oops."

Anna laughed. "Go on. You've been inside too long. Find something outside to do."

"You certain you don't mind?" Miriam asked.

"Scrub the back porch, if you want," Louise suggested. "It doesn't look as though Samuel has thought of that in a while." She pointed to the screen door. "There's another bucket by the pump."

"Go. Go," Anna urged. "Any more women in here and we'll be tripping over each other."

Miriam went out, found a broom and proceeded to

sweep the sand off the porch. She hadn't been at it more than two minutes when Charley shouted to her from the barnyard.

"Morning, Miriam."

"Morning, Charley."

He was raking the barnyard clean of horse droppings, and she assumed that he'd come with the other men to make the farmyard and barn ready for Sunday's gathering. If there was work to be done, you could always count on Charley to be there.

He'd leaned his rake against the barn and started toward the porch, when Miriam heard the sound of a truck engine. As she watched, John pulled up in his truck, with *Hartman Veterinary Services* printed on the side.

"Who's that?" Anna asked as she pushed open the screen door.

"John." Miriam's heart beat faster and she felt a little thrill of excitement. What was he doing here?

Anna snickered. "He was at our house before eight this morning. Is he going to follow you everywhere?"

John blew the horn and waved.

Miriam felt her cheeks grow hot, but she waved back.

"Who is it?" Louise stepped out on the porch behind Anna. "Oh, the vet. Samuel told me that he'd asked him to come. One of his best milkers has a swollen bag. He didn't want it to get worse." She glanced at Anna. "You say he was at your house this morning?"

"He's sweet on Miriam," Anna explained.

Miriam could hear her sister's smile, even if she couldn't see it. "He is not," Miriam protested, sweeping harder. "He came to check on one of our horses. She's developing a hoof infection. John's watching it."

Anna giggled. "More like he's watching you."

"The English yet?" Louise frowned. "Not good." She waggled a finger. "You shouldn't encourage him."

"I'm *not* encouraging him," Miriam said. "We're friends, nothing more."

"He's not English," Anna supplied. "He's Mennonite."

"Ach." Louise shook her head. "Worse, even. You know what they say about those Mennonite boys. Wild, they are."

"Miriam," Mam called from inside the house. "Can you give me a hand with this?"

As she turned to make her escape into the kitchen, Miriam saw Charley walk toward John's truck and lean in the open window. She would have given her best pair of muck boots to hear what those two were saying to each other.

Miriam's eyelids grew heavy. When they drifted shut, Anna poked her hard in the ribs. Miriam gasped, straightened and sat upright. Then she glanced around to see if anyone else had caught her dozing off. Luckily, no one seemed to be watching her.

She was seated on a long backless bench with the other single girls on the women's side of Samuel's parlor. Wide pocket doors allowed a good view of the living room with its chairs for the older members, the bishop and preachers, and guests.

Uncle Reuben was still speaking. The hands on the tall case clock against the staircase read 12:45 p.m. The Sunday service should have been over half an hour ago, and there was still a prayer, the benediction and a final hymn to go. The wooden bench under Miriam was getting harder and harder, and she wiggled to find a more comfortable spot.

Despite the open windows and the breeze, it was warm in the room. She could see Susanna, sitting next to their mother, with her head on Mam's shoulder. Her little sister's face was perspiring and Mam was fanning her. Miriam was warm, too, but not uncomfortably so. It was something else that made her uneasy. The hairs on the back of her neck prickled. She felt as though someone was watching her, but again, when she scanned the two rooms, she saw no one staring in her direction.

Miriam tried to concentrate on her uncle's sermon. He'd been talking about Noah and the hardships of spending so many weeks on the ark during the constant rainfall, but he'd moved on to Jonah and the similarities between the faiths of the two men. Uncle Reuben was known for his long rambling sermons, especially when there were important visitors. She didn't think it was *hochmut* or pride on his part that made him go on so, as much as wanting to put the church in a good light.

She wished he'd get back to Noah's story. Hearing Uncle Reuben tell about Noah gathering the animals had brought back the excitement of the movie Eli had taken her to at the Dover Mall a few months back. She could see the bears and the giraffes and the monkeys, in her mind's eye, climbing the ramp to the ark, two by two, obedient to God's word.

Miriam tried to listen to what her uncle was saying about Jonah, but she still had that feeling that— Charley! Her gazed suddenly settled on him.

He was standing between the main room and the kitchen with a group of his chums, young men who'd come in too late from the barn to be seated, and he was grinning at her. From across two rooms, Miriam could tell that he had been staring at her and that he had seen her falling asleep during Uncle Reuben's sermon. When they made eye contact, he shook his head ever so slightly, obviously admonishing her, that silly grin still on his face. Worse, the other boys had apparently caught her as well. She could tell by the looks on their faces. They were all struggling not to laugh out loud and cause a scene.

Miriam was beside herself. Who knew when they'd come in? Standing in the kitchen doorway, they could slip outside, have a glass of iced tea, grab a slice of pie and then pop back into the sermon without the elders being any the wiser. She'd made a mistake by falling asleep, but mocking her for it was wrong. When she got hold of Charley, she'd tell him so in no uncertain terms.

"Miriam." Anna nudged her again.

Everyone was standing for the benediction and she'd been paying so much attention to Charley and his friends that she'd lost track of where they were in the service. Following the prayer, the deacon announced the date and place of the next service and church ended with a hymn. Miriam and Anna filed out with the unmarried girls and went directly to the kitchen to find an apron and help get the midday meal served.

Since the day was so nice, the young men had assembled the tables outside. Once everyone had left their seats, the boys carried out the benches used in the house for service. Earlier, the girls had set the tables. Now it was a matter of getting the hot food to the tables. The guests, ministers and bishop took their places, followed by the older men and lastly the younger men. The boys and girls would eat at the second seating, so they gathered in groups to talk or ran errands for the women working in the kitchen.

Soon, all the men were eating. Miriam and Anna were assigned the job of carrying pitchers of iced tea, water and milk to the diners. To Miriam's dismay, she found Charley on her side of the table.

"Enjoy your nap?" he whispered.

She poured his glass full of milk. Charley didn't like milk, so it seemed like an act of revenge, even if it was small.

He didn't seem to notice. "Hey, I've got to talk to you later," he continued under his breath. "I've got great news. If you can stay awake until then."

"We saw you," Charley's friend Thomas whispered as he held out his mug for milk. "Sleeping during church, weren't you?"

"I was not," Miriam protested.

"Don't tell lies on Sunday," Charley teased. Then he met her gaze and lowered his voice. "You know I'm just teasing. We've all done it. Meet me later. Wait until you hear."

Miriam passed on to the next man at the table, annoyed with herself for dozing off during the sermon. She'd be hearing about it for weeks from the boys, and sooner or later, it would get to her cousin Dorcas and then to Aunt Martha. Anna should have pinched her to keep her awake.

It wasn't like her to fall asleep during church, although in summer, a lot of the men did. She'd been up since five, and they'd been busy all day yesterday as well. She supposed it was a small sin, but it had been mean of Charley to make more of it than it was. Of course, what could she expect? He always was a tease, making fun of everyone and everything, including himself. Good-time Charley.

It was three hours later when Charley found her and by then, Miriam had almost forgotten her earlier annoyance with him. She was sitting on the side porch with

Johanna's three-year-old on her lap. Jonah had gotten his finger slammed in the screen door by an older child and Miriam was soothing him and applying ice to the boo-boo.

"Here you are." Charley stepped up onto the porch from the lawn. "I've been looking everywhere for you."

"Busy day," she replied, trying to shush Jonah.

Her nephew was still crying on and off and trying to tell her how the accident had happened and how his father had said he was a baby for crying. "*Not* a baby," he protested. "Hurts."

"No, you are not a baby," Miriam agreed. "Katie is the baby and you are the big brother."

"So, what I've been wanting to tell you," Charley started in. "Larry Jones stopped by yesterday. He wants me to work for him full time. Larry's got a contract to work on the hospital addition. I'll have steady masonry work from now on. Isn't that great?"

"Uh-huh," Miriam agreed above the din of the next wave of sobs. "That's wonderful." She stood up with Jonah in her arms. "He mashed his finger in the door. It's a bad pinch, but I don't think anything is broken."

"Hurts," Jonah wailed.

"All right, we'll find your Momma and see what she thinks."

Charley was still looking at her, his face all alight. "Do you know what this means?" he asked. "The steady job?"

"I guess a regular paycheck. That's great." She looked down at her nephew in her arms. "I think I'd best find Johanna. If Jonah gets too upset, he'll throw up his dinner. And he ate a lot of chicken and dumplings, didn't you?" She looked into the little boy's teary eyes as she walked away. "It will be all right. I promise."

"But, Miriam…" Charley said. "I wanted to talk to you…"

"Later," she promised and hurried off with Jonah to find her sister. To her surprise, Charley trailed after her. As she reached the kitchen door, her mother was just coming out with Susanna.

"Jonah got his finger pinched in the door," Miriam explained. "I was looking for Johanna."

"Poor dumpling," Hannah exclaimed, taking him from Miriam. "We'll have to see what we can do about that."

Susanna's eyes widened and her face paled. Miriam knew that her little sister was especially tenderhearted and hated the thought of anyone being in pain.

"Jonah will be fine," Miriam assured Susanna, patting her arm.

Susanna blinked as tears filled her eyes. "Poor Jonah," she said.

Charley cleared his throat. "I have important news, Hannah."

Her mother looked up at him. "*Ya?* Good news, I hope."

"*Ya.* It is." He straightened his shoulders. "Larry Jones wants me to work with him on the new wing for the hospital. I'll have steady work."

"Excellent," Mam said, shifting the little boy to her hip. "You're a good mason. They couldn't have anyone more dependable."

"Oh, there's Johanna," Miriam said as she caught sight of her sister coming into the kitchen from the pantry. "Johanna. Jonah needs you."

Mam carried Jonah inside where he was immediately surrounded by sympathetic mothers, aunts and grandmothers. By the time Miriam glanced back over her shoulder to speak to Charley again, he had retreated to male territory in the barnyard.

It was after six when Mam, Miriam, Susanna and Anna walked across the pasture toward home. It had been a busy day, but a satisfying one. There were still cows to be milked, eggs to be gathered, chickens and pigs to feed and water, but Miriam actually looked forward to it. This was a good time, chatting with Mam and Anna, remembering the laughter and shared worship of another peaceful Sunday.

"It's good that Charley got steady work," Mam said.

"Uh-huh," Miriam agreed. "He certainly was excited about it."

Anna rolled her eyes. "I wonder why."

"Well, he would be pleased," Miriam said. "He didn't have much work last winter. People weren't doing much building around Dover."

"He made a special point of telling Mam about the job," Anna reminded her.

"So?" Miriam frowned. This teasing about Charley and her was getting a little annoying.

"Hey, Miriam!" Irwin called. He'd gone on ahead to get a start on the chores. Now, he climbed up a fence and waved. "Your boyfriend's here!"

Anna glanced at Mam. "I wonder which one?"

"That's not funny," Miriam said, but she quickened her step, wondering who Irwin was talking about.

As if he'd read her mind, Irwin shouted. "It's John. He wants to see Miriam in the barn."

"I'm coming," Miriam called, then turned back to her mother. "He must have stopped to see Molly on his way home."

"Two times he comes on a Sunday?" Mam didn't

sound particularly pleased. "Susanna, go with your sister."

Miriam glanced at her mother, not certain she'd heard her mother correctly. "It's just John," she said. "I told you Molly's leg was warm this morning and we're concerned about an infection. Why do I need Susanna—?"

"Two times to come on his day off," Mam repeated, setting her mouth the way she did when there would be no changing her mind. "You do as I say, Miriam. Take your sister with you. See to the horse and nothing more. I am lenient with you girls because I trust you, but we'll give the neighbors no cause for scandal."

Chapter Five

"Wait," Susanna cried. "Wait for me. Mam said I have to come with you." Her short legs pumped as she tried to catch up. "Wait, Miriam."

Miriam stopped and tried to compose herself. When Susanna reached her, she took her little sister's hand and smiled at her. "You're getting faster," she said.

Susanna grinned. "Mam said that I'm s'posed to—"

"*Ya,*" Miriam agreed. She let go of Susanna's hand and straightened her sister's *kapp.* "You like John, don't you?"

Susanna nodded, and Miriam caught her hand again. Together they walked toward the barn. Miriam could feel Mam's gaze boring into her back, but she didn't look back.

Maybe Anna is right, Miriam thought. *Maybe he is coming to see me.* A delicious shiver passed through her. She had to admit that thinking of John as more than a friend was exciting. But it was scary at the same time. She'd never considered that an English boy might be attracted to her. Of course, being a Mennonite, John really wasn't an Englisher, but he wasn't Amish, either. The church would frown on anything beyond the friendship she and John had right now, even if she wanted it to be more. It would be wrong, wouldn't it?

But then, God did work in mysterious ways. Ruth and Eli were proof of that. Who would ever have thought the bad boy Eli Lapp would have been the right boy for her sister, and yet with every passing day, Miriam was more sure he was. What if God had a plan for Miriam that was just as unexpected? What if it was God's plan for her that she not live her life in the old way?

The idea intrigued her. There were so many things about the outside world that called to her. The possibility of more education was the first that came to mind. If she got a high school diploma, could she work in an animal hospital? Could she become an animal technician?

She pushed open the barn door and held it for Susanna. Inside, it was cooler. "Hello, John," she called. "Here we are."

He stood up, removed his baseball cap, ran his hand through his hair, and put the hat back on. "I thought you'd be home from church earlier."

"We stayed to help clean up and to visit."

"Ya," Susanna chimed in. "We had chocolate cake and ginger cookies."

They walked through the barn to join John in Molly's stall. The mare was contentedly chewing a mouthful of new hay. "How is she doing?" Miriam asked, stroking the horse's neck.

John patted Molly's rump. "Good girl," he murmured.

His gaze met Miriam's, and she knew instinctively, that whatever concern he had for the horse, he'd come to see her as well. She waited.

Outside, in the pound, the cows mooed. It was past time for milking. They'd stayed too long at Samuel's.

Any minute, Irwin and Anna would be here to help with evening chores. "Is Molly worse?"

"Her hoof doesn't seem any worse than this morning," he answered, "but it really isn't any better, either."

"I'm applying the medicine exactly as you told me," Miriam assured him. She couldn't help thinking how cute he was, and how not-Amish he looked in his jeans and long-sleeve T-shirt and green ball cap that read *John Deere.*

"Ya," Susanna said. "Miriam's making Molly better. I love Molly."

John looked at Susanna and then back at Miriam, and she realized that he wanted to tell her something without her sister hearing.

Miriam glanced at Susanna. "I think Molly needs a new mineral block." She picked up the remains of the one in her feed box. "There's a new one in the feed room. Could you get it, Susanna?"

Her sister nodded and hurried away, eager to help, as always.

Miriam felt a small twinge of guilt to have deceived Susanna to get her out of the way, but she trusted John. If it was bad news, Miriam would want to pick the time and the place to tell Susanna. She crumpled a corner of her apron into a ball and glanced at him expectantly. "Molly isn't worse, is she?"

"It feels like the hoof is heating up. Here." He crouched down beside the mare and laid his hand gently on Molly's leg just above the hoof.

Miriam crouched beside him and then he surprised her by grabbing her hand. She didn't know what to do. It was warm and big and—

"Right here." He pressed her hand to the same spot he'd just touched. "Feel it?"

He was so close, she could smell fabric softener. Even though his jeans were dirty from being in barns, his shirt was clean. He'd put on a clean shirt before coming.

Miriam tried to block out John and just feel what he was trying to get her to feel. Molly's leg was definitely warm. "*Ya*. I feel it."

He stood up, reached into his pocket and pulled out a small red cell phone. "I was thinking. In case she spikes a fever, or if you needed to ask me—anything…about her treatment. If you had questions." He passed her the phone. "I want you to have this."

She stared at the cell phone in her hand. It was a lot smaller than a deck of cards and so bright that it almost glowed. "A phone?"

Some of the boys who considered themselves *rum-springa*—in their running around years—had phones but Miriam didn't know any girls who did—at least not in Kent County. Telephones weren't allowed by the *Ordnung,* the church rules.

"I don't know," she hedged. She wanted the phone badly. She'd always been fascinated by them. It was so tempting to take it. John was right. If there was a problem in the night with Molly, she could reach him right away, instead of walking to the chair shop and using the phone there.

"It's okay, right? For something like this? I don't want to get you in trouble." His brow furrowed and she saw how concerned he was for her. "This is the power button. You push that and then hit #1. I programmed in my number. To send, you hit this button."

"I know how they work," she assured him. "I see the English customers using them all the time at Spence's and in the stores." She hesitated, feeling the weight of the phone in her hand.

"I thought…since you haven't officially joined the church yet, it would be okay. You having the phone." He sounded nervous. But in a good way.

"*Ya,* that's true," she said. Having a cell phone or using it to call the vet wasn't really against the *Ordnung.* Since she hadn't joined the church, she wasn't bound by the same restrictions that baptized members were.

When the accident happened, no one thought it was wrong to use the phone at the chair shop to call the vet. In fact, the objection to telephones was the phone wires that connected them to the English world, not the actual phone. A cell phone didn't have a wire.

Miriam stared at the phone in her hand. She knew she didn't have much time. Susanna would be back, and if she saw the phone, she'd tell everyone about it. That was the bad thing about her little sister. Whatever Susanna knew, she repeated it to anyone she spoke to. And nothing Miriam could say would make her understand that her having a phone wasn't a sin—or that she didn't have to tell Mam about it.

"So this would just be for calling you if Molly got worse?" Her heart was pounding so hard that she was afraid that John could hear it. *Say no,* she told herself. She looked at him.

He took her hand with both of his, cradling hers, cradling the cell phone. His hand felt warmer than the phone and Miriam felt a thrill run to the tips of her toes. This close to him again, she felt almost dizzy.

"I'd be lying if I said it was just for the mare," John admitted. "I like you a lot. And I want you to call me whenever you want." He squeezed her hand and then released it. "We're friends." He hesitated. "But I think it's more than friends, Miriam. I think we're past that."

"You're Mennonite," she said, so softly that it was barely a whisper.

"I know."

"And I'm Amish."

"Yes."

"There would be problems."

"You're right."

"It wouldn't be easy, if we…"

He shook his head. "No, it wouldn't, but we should see, don't you think? We should find out if…if it *is* more than friendship."

"I've got the block." Susanna held it high as she skipped toward them from the feed room.

A stray chicken squawked and scurried out of Susanna's way.

"Close the door so the rats can't get in," Miriam shouted to her sister. Dat had lined the whole feed room in sheets of tin to keep out vermin. Even the door was mouseproof.

"You have to tell me if you want to keep it, Miriam. I know you want to," John pressed quietly. "Will you take it?"

She looked up into his eyes and a bubble of mischief rose in her chest. She'd always been a little rebellious. She'd ridden horses when girls weren't supposed to. She'd played ball with the boys and walked the ridgepole on the barn when everyone else was afraid to.

"Dare you," John challenged.

She slipped the red cell phone into her apron pocket. "If Mam finds out, I'll be in big trouble."

"Me, too." He chuckled, and she laughed with him.

It would be their secret, Miriam thought. She couldn't wait to try out the phone, to talk to him in the night. Just the thought of calling him on the little red phone made her face feel warm. *This is temptation,* she thought. But will it lead to something more? Only time would tell.

"Here you go." Susanna walked into the stall, carrying the mineral block.

"Good work." John looked at Miriam and then back at Susanna, again. "You're a big help, Susanna, the best." He patted Molly's withers. "I guess I'd best be getting on home," he said. "I have an early call in Felton."

"Ya," Miriam agreed. "I have to get to the milking. It's late."

"I leave the house at about seven," he said. "And it takes me about twenty minutes to get there." He was telling her to call him. *Tomorrow.*

"Seven," she repeated, already planning how she could get away—maybe into the old milk house that served as a library. The walls were thick there. She could make her call from there and no one would hear.

"Mam says get on with the milking," Irwin called, banging open the barn door.

Miriam looked up, noting that Irwin hadn't said Hannah but Mam. It was the first time she'd heard him refer to her mother as Mam.

"Before they burst," Irwin continued. He stopped and scowled at John. "Out late, aren't you?"

"I was on my way home from another call. Just thought I'd check on Molly." If John thought he was being rude, he didn't act like it.

"Never saw so much fuss over a hoof," Irwin grumbled. "I'll let the cows in, Miriam."

"'Night," John said, walking away. "Talk to you soon, Miriam."

She nodded. "Soon." The phone in her apron pocket pressed hot against her thigh. "Thanks for stopping by."

She knew that her mother would not approve of her taking it, but she also knew she'd make that call to John tomorrow morning.

"Hello, is this John?" Miriam asked loudly. It was 7:15 a.m. on Monday, and she'd ducked into the old milk house. She was so nervous that her hands were shaking.

He laughed. "You punched in my number. Who else would it be?"

The radio music in the background ended abruptly and Miriam guessed that John had turned it off.

"Are you still there?" he asked.

"*Ya*, I'm here." She held the cell phone tightly. All night she'd kept thinking of things that they'd talk about, and now that she'd actually reached him, her mind had gone blank. It felt so strange, using a phone just to talk. She had plenty of experience using phones; she called to make appointments for people all the time. But this was different.

"How's Molly?"

"Good. Same as last night." She peered out the window, hoping that Irwin or Anna wouldn't discover her here. If they did, what reason could she give for being in the library so early? What she was doing wasn't hurting anyone, but it was private. And if there was one thing difficult to find growing up in a house with six sisters and an observant mother, it was privacy.

"Hoof infections are tricky. She's not out of the woods yet," John said.

She could picture him at the wheel of the truck, a bottle of root beer in one hand. John liked his soda. He always bought one for himself and one for her when they shared lunch at Spence's. She began to relax a little. "What is your call this morning? You said you were going to Felton."

"Oh, just routine immunizations. It's a horse farm. Trotters. They want me to certify a two-year-old for sale. He's going to Tennessee."

Once the talk turned to horses, it was easy to fall into a comfortable conversation with John. She liked the way that he treated her as an equal, as if she understood everything. Most of it, she did.

"I was wondering," he said.

"*Ya,* of what?"

"Wednesday I have to drive to Easton to pick up something for my grandfather. There's a nice little restaurant over there. Maybe you could go with me, just for the ride."

Like a date, she thought. Was she ready for that? First the cell phone and then sneaking off for the day with him. Mam would never give her permission, not unless she took one of her sisters with her, and probably not then. But was it wrong to want to go with John? They'd had lunch together lots of times at Spence's. What would make that all right and going with him to Easton the wrong choice?

"I can't," she said. "We're making applesauce with Johanna on Wednesday." That wasn't really a lie. Mam had mentioned that they might do that one day this week. Maybe she wasn't ready to take such a big step, or maybe the thought of sneaking behind Mam's back made her feel small and mean.

"Maybe another time, then."

"Maybe," she agreed. She could imagine him pulling off his ball cap and running his hand through his short hair, the way he did when he didn't know what to say. A lump rose in her throat. She didn't want to do anything to hurt her friendship with John, but she didn't want to betray her mother's trust, either. "I think I had better go. They'll wonder where I am."

"All right. It was nice talking to you. Can you call me again tonight?"

"What time?" She lowered her voice.

She could hear Irwin calling to Jeremiah. Irwin always played with the little terrier in the morning before chores. Irwin would throw a stick and Jeremiah would run after it, then Irwin would try to get the dog to bring the stick back. But the ragtag little terrier had ideas of his own and he'd tease Irwin by running circles around him. It was a fun game, but Irwin and the dog could spend a half hour fooling around when there were chores to be done.

"Ten?" John suggested.

Miriam shook her head. "Too late. I share a bedroom with my sister, and I'd have to sneak out. How about nine?"

"Ok, nine it is. Wait, will you be at Spence's tomorrow?"

"*Ya*. At least this week. We have eggs and jams to sell."

"I'll see you there, then."

"I have to go, John. 'Bye." She hit the Off button.

Now, what to do with the phone? She didn't want to carry it around all day with her. What if it fell out of her pocket? What if Anna or Ruth noticed the bulge and asked what it was?

She climbed on Susanna's chair and pushed the red phone back on the top shelf, then slid a book on Pennsylvania Dutch Recipes in front of it. The book was old and tattered and had once been sold to tourists. Mam said the recipes weren't very good, but Aunt Martha had donated the book, so it had to go in the library.

She got down off the chair and looked at the book. No one had borrowed it since the library opened, and if they did, Susanna would knock the book down with the broom handle Irwin had found for her. No one would ever see the red cell phone and no one would know that she was secretly calling John Hartman.

Miriam crossed her fingers and said a prayer that they wouldn't.

As she and Anna began setting up their sale table at Spence's Bazaar the following morning, Miriam glanced around anxiously for John. She'd told him that she'd call last night, but she hadn't been able to think of an excuse to get away. They'd had a family emergency.

What would she say to him? She couldn't share family problems with John, but neither did she want him to think that she'd promise to call and just not do it. She wondered if he would act differently if he did show up. Would Anna suspect that something more than their usual friendship was going on? Would she be able to talk to John as easily as they had in the past? Her stomach knotted. She'd not been able to eat this morning. Instead of her normal hearty breakfast, she'd had a slice of toast and a cup of coffee. If this was what romance was, she wasn't certain that it was as much fun as everyone insinuated.

And, besides worrying about John, she couldn't get Johanna out of her mind. Johanna and the children had showed up at the back door just as they were finishing supper last night. Johanna's eyes were red and Miriam suspected that she'd been crying, but her oldest sister would never admit such a thing. Johanna had asked her and the others to watch the children. She said she needed to talk to Mam. Naturally, they all wanted to know what was wrong, but Johanna was the stubborn one. Whatever her problem was, no one would know until she was ready to reveal it.

Mam and Johanna had spent the better part of two hours together in Mam's bedroom. Miriam had wanted to find some excuse to creep down the hall and listen at the door, but she'd never do such a thing. She had to respect Johanna's privacy, but it wasn't easy. She, Ruth and Anna were all worried. Only Susanna was her normal happy self, rocking baby Katie in the big rocker Dat's father had handcrafted until the baby had drifted off to sleep.

It had been after nine when Mam had asked Miriam to hitch Blackie to the courting buggy and drive Johanna and the baby home. Mam had tucked Jonah into her bed and promised that someone would drop him off in the morning. Miriam had tried to find out what was wrong, but Johanna remained tight-lipped. When they'd gotten down from the carriage at Johanna's house, everything was dark.

"Pray for our family," Johanna had said as she'd carried a sleeping Katie up her back steps.

"But, are you all right? Are you sick?" Miriam had called after her in a hushed voice. "Is something—?"

"Just pray for me, sister. God has a plan for us. I know He does."

Miriam and Anna had discussed Johanna on the buggy ride to Dover this morning, but Anna didn't seem to know much more than she did. "It's a problem with Wilmer," Anna said. "Not sickness, at least not of the body. He's strong as a plow horse. But I don't think it is a happy marriage."

None of them had really liked Wilmer Detweiler when he'd started coming around the house. He had a steady job in construction and he was a faithful member of the church, but he was moody. Miriam, especially, couldn't see why fun-loving Johanna would be attracted to him. Everyone had thought that Johanna and Charley's older brother Roland had been courting for two years, but they'd apparently argued and then broken up. As usual, no one had been able to pry anything out of Johanna.

But if Johanna and Wilmer's marriage was in trouble, that was serious. They had two children together, and among the Plain people, marriage was a sacred bond made before God. The couple became one when they took their vows and there was no breaking that union. Marriage was for life.

"Miriam!"

Two jars of strawberry jam toppled out of the basketful that she was carrying from the back of the buggy to the table. Anna caught them both before they hit the ground.

"Whoa, easy," Anna said. "Pay attention to what you're doing, twin. We spent too many hours making that jam to waste it."

"Ya," Miriam agreed. Lucky that Anna, despite her size, was so quick. "I was thinking about Johanna and Wilmer."

Anna nodded and her cinnamon-brown eyes watered up. "On my knees, last night, I prayed for them."

Across the drive, Aunt Martha and Dorcas had a display of fall flowers for sale along with the wooden toys Uncle Reuben made in his spare time. There was a Noah's ark and an array of animals, a simple sailboat with a long string so that a child could sail it and a girl's market basket with wooden eggs, vegetables and cups and saucers, all painted to look real.

Aunt Martha and Uncle Reuben's farm wasn't as productive as many others in the community; they'd always had to struggle, but they worked hard every day. Miriam hoped Uncle Reuben would find customers for his toys. Most English children, it seemed, wanted electronic toys that blinked and squealed and flashed, rather than simple handmade items.

Miriam was putting a quart of grapes on the table when suddenly someone came up behind her and put their hands over her eyes.

"Stop it." Embarrassed, she pulled at the hands. It was a man, not a woman. "Let me go," she said. She could imagine everyone staring at her.

"You have to guess first," Anna said with a giggle from beside her.

"John."

"Wrong." Charley took his hands down and stepped back.

Miriam whipped around and looked from him to Anna. She could feel her face growing hot. She wanted to run away and hide.

"Just me," Charley said with a frown of obvious disappointment. "Just good old Charley."

Miriam could hear Dorcas laughing behind her. "Charley, I didn't—"

"If you were looking for John, you didn't miss by much," he said. He wasn't smiling now. Hurt showed in his eyes, and his voice was tight. "Here comes your Mennonite boy now."

Chapter Six

"Hey, Charley, here comes trouble," shouted Harvey Borntrager. He and two other Amish boys were leaning against the wall of the poultry shed. Harvey laughed and gestured toward John Hartman, walking toward the Yoder stall carrying a cardboard tray of hot drinks.

Charley pushed his straw hat back on his head with an index finger and glared at Harvey. "That's enough," he warned. He'd taken the morning off from working on Eli's house, hoping to get a chance to talk to Miriam alone, and now, here came John again. It wasn't fair, but no matter how out-of-sorts he was with Miriam, he wouldn't stand by and let Harvey and his gang poke fun at him.

"Just looking out for your interest," Harvey said.

"Mind your own business, or you'll have me to deal with later," Charley warned. He glanced back at Miriam. "So, I guess I'm the third wheel here, right?"

Miriam shoved the quart basket of grapes across the table and hurriedly pushed another after it. She turned abruptly to face him. "What are you talking about?"

"Him. People think you like John, maybe more than you should."

"That's not fair."

"Maybe it is and maybe it isn't."

"Don't make a fuss, Charley. Everybody's looking at us."

"I guess they are. Maybe with good reason." He could feel her aunt Martha's eyes boring into his back. He glanced over his shoulder and Dorcas waved.

"Morning, Charley," Dorcas called.

"Morning," he said, before turning back to Miriam. He raised his gaze to meet hers directly. She looked as if she were about to burst into tears. Suddenly, his anger drained away. The thought of making Miriam cry was worse than attempting to explain how confused he felt about her friendship with John. "I guess I'll see you later."

She nodded.

He turned, straightened his back and walked directly toward John.

"Morning, Charley." John grinned and held up the tray. "Coffee? I've got extra."

"Ne."

He wanted to have it out with John right here, to tell him to stay away from his girl, but it wasn't the Amish way. The Bible taught that a man should be kind to his neighbors, that he shouldn't harbor bad thoughts in his heart. That went for everyone, including Mennonites and Englishers. It was probably nothing but jealousy and John hadn't done anything wrong. He had to keep reminding himself that Miriam was Amish. She'd never look at someone from another faith. Nothing John could do or say could steal her away from the Plain people.

"Got to do something," Charley muttered as he hurried past John. He couldn't stand here and watch Miriam laughing and talking with him. He'd find her before she left the auction and they'd have that talk. He'd make her see how he felt.

Charley's abrupt behavior puzzled John. It was clear that something had upset him. He wondered if he and Miriam had argued. Did the Amish argue? He supposed they must, like anyone else, but he'd never seen anything but gentle speech between them. Oh, men could be rowdy, even tell off-color jokes, but as a rule they seemed to possess an inner calm. He wished he could say that about himself.

"Good morning," Anna called. "Is that coffee I smell?" She giggled. "I told Miriam you were bringing us hot coffee."

"Indeed, I am," John said. "And some raisin buns."

Anna reached for one. "Sticky buns, yum. My favorite."

"Coffee, Miriam?" He held up a paper cup. "Milk and one sugar. Is that right?"

"Ya." She nodded. Her hand trembled as she took the coffee. "Thank you."

Anna giggled again. "Thank you, Dr. John. I missed my second cup at breakfast."

An egg customer approached and John stood aside as Miriam waited on her. "I'd like to buy some of your blueberry jam for Uncle Albert," he said when the English woman had moved on to look at the next table. "He loves it."

"We've got plenty," Anna said. "Eight dollars for a pint, five for the half-pint. And we've got strawberry, as well. Miriam made the strawberry."

He smiled at Miriam. "In that case, I'd better have three large jars of each."

"That's a lot of jam," Miriam said, beginning to put jars into a plastic bag. "You don't need to buy so much."

"But I do," he assured her. He wanted to ask her why she hadn't called him last night, to tell her that he'd waited to hear from her, but he didn't want to say anything about the cell phone in front of Anna. "We need something to make breakfast edible," he finished. "Something tasty."

"Then I'll put in a jar of honey, no charge," Miriam said. "Because you're such a good customer."

"I'd better get some more jam out of the buggy." Anna went to the carriage, opened the small door in the back and began to rummage in the cardboard boxes.

"I waited for you to call," John whispered, when Anna was too far away to hear. "What happened?"

"I can't talk now." Miriam glanced across at her aunt Martha's stand. "I'll be in trouble."

"Can you have lunch with me?"

"If Anna comes, too."

"All right. Meet me inside at one."

"Not inside," Miriam said. "Too many people."

Her cheeks were flushed as pink as her lips, and a few curls had escaped from her *kapp*. John was struck again by just how pretty she was. She didn't wear a dab of makeup and her simple green dress had a high neck and long sleeves. But he found her fresh and adorable from the toes of her sensible black athletic shoes to the crown of her bonneted head. "Where, then? The picnic tables under the trees?"

"All right," she agreed. "Now take your jam and go before Aunt Martha comes over and chases you away."

He chuckled. "She would, too, wouldn't she?"

"I'm afraid so."

* * *

As John was leaving, an older couple trailed by a little girl stopped to ask Miriam about eggs. The woman was dressed in pink sweats with shiny pink and white sneakers, and the man had a mustache and a big belly that hung over his Bermuda shorts. He was carrying a tiny white poodle with a blue bow and blue toenails. The child, wearing a pink tutu, a rhinestone-studded top that read *Hot Chick* and silver flip-flops, waved a blue, half-eaten lollypop nearly as large as her head.

"Are these eggs organic?" the woman demanded in a loud voice. "I only buy eggs from free-range chickens." By her accent, Miriam thought she might be from Jersey City or New York.

"I want ice cream," the child whined. "You said I could have ice cream." She threw her lollypop into the dirt, kicked it under the table and then began to yank on the woman's sleeve.

"Stop that, Melody. Be nice."

The dog snapped at the child.

"Ice cream after lunch," the man said. "Are...your eggs...white...or brown?"

He had the same accent as the woman, but he spoke in an artificially choppy manner to Miriam, as if he were trying to make himself understood in a foreign country without speaking the language.

"Why is she wearing that funny hat?" the little girl demanded.

"She's a Quaker," the woman explained. "They have to dress like that."

"White or brown?" the man repeated loudly.

Miriam gestured at the open carton of large brown eggs on display and wondered if he was color-blind. She knew that she should answer his question, but she was afraid that if she opened her mouth, she might burst into laughter.

"Ice cream!"

The dog began to yip.

"She's not a Quaker. She's Aim-ish," the man corrected. "Merle said this was an Aim-ish market."

"Chocolate!"

"You prefer white eggs." The woman ignored the now-screaming child. "I'm not sure you'd like brown. What do they eat?"

Miriam gritted her teeth. Did the woman want to know what the chickens ate or the eggs ate? She was still thinking about Charley and John and what Aunt Martha would just have to report to Mam, but she couldn't afford to offend customers, even rude ones who thought she was deaf.

"They only speak Pennsylvania Dutch, Mildred," the man said. "Don't you?" He raised his voice and the dog barked louder. "You speak Dutch?"

"Ice cream!" the child demanded and began to kick the woman's ankle.

"Can I help you?" Anna bustled up to the table wearing her widest smile. "I speak English."

Gratefully, Miriam let her sister deal with the tourists while she hurried back to the horse and smothered her laughter in Blackie's neck. Most of the people she dealt with at the sale were pleasant, but some were so ignorant they were just silly.

Sales for the next two hours were good. They sold all the eggs and jam and even took an order for one of Johanna's custom-made quilts. As it neared one o'clock, Miriam and Anna packed up the few items that hadn't sold, watered Blackie and strolled over to find an empty picnic table in the shade. As usual, Anna had packed a big lunch. There would be more than enough fried chicken, potato salad, deviled eggs and brownies to share with John.

He was already seated at the weathered table when they arrived. Miriam smiled when she saw that he'd brought sodas and a pizza and spread newspapers out to make a clean place to eat. "We've got enough for you to take home for dinner," she teased. "Then you won't have to eat Uncle Albert's cooking tonight."

"Amen to that," John said.

Anna laughed. "Maybe you should learn to cook, John."

"No, I'll leave that to you girls. It's all I can do to boil an egg."

"You don't boil eggs," Anna retorted with a twitter. "You just bring them to a simmer, turn them off and put the lid on. You let them cook in hot water, not boil them. Makes green streaks if you boil them."

Miriam took a seat across the table from John and he passed her a root beer. "How was your morning?" she asked.

He began to tell her about the calf he'd gone to tend as Anna dug in to the pizza. Miriam nibbled on a chicken leg. It was nice here, sitting in the shade, laughing and talking. She felt comfortable with John, as though she belonged here in the outside world. Her family and community might consider him an outsider, but he didn't seem like that to her. There were other people around them at tables, a few Amish but mostly English. No one seemed to be paying any attention to the three of them, as though it was perfectly normal for friends of different faiths to share lunch and laughter.

Nearby, a truck radio blared country music and John tapped the table in time to the rhythm. Miriam was having a wonderful time, eating pizza and drinking her soda pop, until Charley and two of his buddies walked up.

"Something looks good," Titus said. "Is that your chicken, Anna?"

Anna looked at Titus, averted her eyes and blushed. "Help yourself," she offered, waving to the feast spread out on the newspapers. There's extra paper plates and plastic forks."

His brother Menno reached for a drumstick and took a seat at the table next to Anna.

"And there's plenty of pizza," John offered. "Charley?"

Charley shook his head. "Not hungry."

"No, sit down and join us," Miriam said, suddenly uncomfortable. "We're having lunch."

Charley hooked a thumb in the waistband of his jeans. "I can see that."

Miriam's embarrassment changed to annoyance. Charley was being deliberately difficult. She didn't want to hurt Charley's feelings, but he had no right to act this way. He was making a big thing of her friendship with John, almost as if he were jealous and doing it in front of Menno and Titus.

But then she remembered that he'd told her he wanted to talk to her. He'd tried to talk to her after church and again later on Sunday. She couldn't imagine what he had to tell her, since he'd already shared his news about the new job, but she didn't want to be unkind. "Charley was hired to work on the new construction at the hospital," she said.

John smiled. "Glad to hear it."

"Steady work," Titus said. "I've got a job there, too."

"You're both masons, aren't you?" John asked.

"*Ya.*" Titus pushed a forkful of potato salad into his mouth. "Charley's uncle taught us both the trade. It pays good."

Anna glanced up at Titus, saw him grinning at her and blushed until her cheeks looked like she'd stained them with beet juice. Miriam knew that her sister liked Titus, but he was a good-looking boy, popular with all the girls. And Charley's sister, Mary, had said that Titus was walking out with a girl from one of the neighboring Amish churches.

Miriam didn't know if Menno had a girlfriend, but she doubted that he'd be interested in Anna, either. As much as she loved her twin sister, she was afraid that Anna was too Plain for the boys their age. Most young men, like the English boys, went for cute girls.

John passed a slice of pizza to Titus. Soon everyone was talking and sharing the lunch, all but Charley. He just stood at the end of the table watching Miriam as if he expected her to say something. The trouble was, she didn't know what she was supposed to say.

"I guess we'd better get home," Anna said when they'd finished most of the food. "I don't think we left enough for your family for supper, John."

"That's all right. I'll pick up some sandwiches."

Charley pushed his hat back. "Are you coming to Ruth and Eli's house-raising Saturday?"

He glanced at Miriam, then back at Charley. "Am I invited?"

Charley shrugged his broad shoulders. "Anybody's welcome. At least anybody who knows one end of a hammer from the other. But I guess they don't teach that in college, do they?"

It was John's turn to stiffen and flush to the roots of his hair. "Not at vet school, at least," he answered as he rose to his feet. "But I can probably muddle through. All right if I come, Miriam?"

"We would be pleased to have you," Anna said quickly.

Miriam scowled at Charley. "We start early. Seven. And don't bring lunch. We'll have plenty at noon."

"*Ya.*" Anna glanced up at Titus through her lashes and smiled. "Plenty of food."

"I have to warn you." Charley shook his head. "It's hard work, raising a house. You may get blisters on those soft hands."

Menno chuckled.

"Don't worry about me, Charley." John seemed to throw back his narrower shoulders. "I'll be there on time and I'll outwork you."

Titus groaned. "These Mennonite boys can be touchy."

For long seconds the air across the picnic table seemed charged with energy and then Charley grinned. "We'll see about that, college boy," he said. "Bring a hammer if you have one." He walked away. "Come on, fellows. I think the cow auction is starting. We wouldn't want to miss anything."

Miriam glared at him. "No, I guess you wouldn't."

John watched as the three walked away across the parking lot. "I want to come to the house-raising, Miriam, but I don't want to make trouble for your family."

"There won't be any trouble," she answered softly. "I don't know what's gotten into Charley. He's not usually like that."

"He's jealous of you and Miriam," Anna told John.

"It was just lunch," Miriam protested. But she knew that wasn't quite true. There was more between her and John than friendship, and Charley had seen it.

Later, on the ride home in the buggy, Anna brought

up Charley's rude behavior. "He's jealous, I tell you," she said. "And I'd say Charley has good reason."

"That's silly," Miriam argued, fingering the leather reins in her hands.

"What's silly is my sister has two beaus and I can't get one. How fair is that, I ask you?"

"Stop it. I don't have two beaus."

"You like John." Anna gazed at her earnestly. "Can you deny it?"

"What if I did?"

"It will cause trouble, twin. Mam's Amish now, she thinks Amish. She won't let you run off with a Mennonite. You can count on that. Best you take Charley and be happy with him."

"But I don't love Charley," Miriam said, slapping the lines over Blackie's back so that the gelding broke into a fast trot and the buggy swayed back and forth. "If you like him so well, you take him."

"Gladly," Anna replied sadly. "But we both know that he'd not have me. When I get a husband, *if* I get a husband, he'll be seventy years old with a beard down to his waist and an Adam's apple the size of your *kapp*."

Miriam softened and reached out to pat her sister's hand. "That's not true, Anna." She hesitated. "But what's wrong with John? He's sweet."

"Sweet he may be and easy on the eyes, but he's not Plain. I can't see you going against the family and the church to marry a Mennonite." Anna leaned back on the buggy seat, folding her arms over her ample bosom. "You're playing with fire, if you ask me."

"Maybe I am," Miriam conceded. "But I don't want to settle. I want what Mam and Dat had…what Ruth and Eli have. I want a love that will last forever."

"And can a Mennonite boy give you that?"

"Not a *Mennonite boy*. John. John Hartman. He's a good man, Anna."

"Do you love him?"

"I don't know." Miriam pressed her lips tightly together. "I guess I just want a chance to find out."

Chapter Seven

After Miriam and Ruth finished milking that evening, Miriam ducked back into the milk house to recover the cell phone. When she turned it on, she saw that it indicated three missed calls—all from John. She didn't want to try and reach him now because she was expected in the kitchen to help put supper on the table. Neither did she feel at ease leaving the phone here. She knew it wasn't logical, but all day, she'd kept worrying that Susanna would find some reason to collect a book off the top shelf and somehow discover the phone.

In some ways, Susanna was a child, but in others, she was smart. She'd recognize the cell phone for what it was and take it straight to Mam. In fact, she wouldn't even wait until Mam got home; she'd probably march it straight to the schoolhouse and tell Mam right in front of all the children, and then everyone in the community would know. Cell phones were not strictly forbidden by the *Ordnung,* because there were no wires or lines connecting the phone to the English world. Some of the men, especially those who had businesses, carried cell phones, but she didn't know of a single woman in Kent County who had one.

She didn't need another thing to worry about. All day she'd been going over what had happened at lunchtime with Charley. The look on his face had really upset her. It bothered her that she had obviously hurt his feelings, but what right did Charley have to be jealous of John? Charley wasn't her boyfriend. Why was he being so difficult? It had been both unlike him and unkind to tease John about his carpentry skills. Yes, John had an education. What was wrong with that? How could he be a veterinarian if he hadn't gone to school for so long? It was unfair to give John a hard time about choices he'd made in his life, especially when their whole community depended on John and his uncle and grandfather.

Her friendship with John meant a lot. And if it was more than friendship, if it was the beginning of something more, she had the right to pursue it, didn't she? Mam would be the first one to urge her to follow her heart, wouldn't she? Hadn't she given up her own faith to become Amish for Dat? And hadn't she found peace and love in the Amish community? What if God had the same intentions for Miriam?

She wanted to ask her mother for advice, but Mam already had so much else on her mind with the wedding and Johanna and the troubles with *Grossmama*. And at some point, Miriam felt as if she had to begin making some of her own decisions. If she was old enough to be thinking about becoming a wife, and God willing a mother, wasn't she old enough to begin making her own decisions?

"Miriam?" Anna called from the back porch.

Miriam glanced back at the top shelf, wondering if she should return the phone to its hiding place, then decided against.

"Miriam! Supper!"

That was Mam. And it didn't pay to be late to the table; Mam didn't tolerate tardiness without a good explanation.

Miriam dropped the cell into the deep pocket of her apron, hurried out of the milk house and up to the house.

"What kept you?" Ruth asked when she walked into the kitchen. She was studying her with an expression that said she knew Miriam was up to something.

Miriam put a finger to her lips and silently formed the word, *"Later."*

Ruth scowled, but let it drop.

The household wouldn't be the same once her big sister moved into her own home with Eli. Even though Ruth would only be across the field, Miriam would miss her terribly. She wondered if she should confide in Ruth about the phone, but thought better of it. Ruth already had too much on her mind, too, with the coming wedding and the house construction. This should be a happy time, not one in which she need worry about Miriam's silly little problems.

The delicious odor of potato soup filled the big kitchen. After she'd gotten home from school, Mam had fired up her much beloved black and nickel wood-burning cookstove, made the soup using last night's leftover potatoes and baked a pan of biscuits and three apple pies. Keeping the oven temperature just right on the cookstove was tricky, and Miriam and Ruth much preferred the modern gas range that ran on propane. Fortunately, their kitchen was large enough for both stoves and having two came in handy when there was a lot of baking to do.

Irwin was already at the table, hair slicked straight back and smelling of hair tonic. Miriam noticed that his straw-colored hair needed cutting again. Irwin was still small for his age, but his hair and ears seemed to grow faster than anyone else Miriam knew. She had to admit that, despite his skinny frame, he was a much more attractive boy than he'd been when he'd first come to live in Delaware.

Mam never did things halfway. Strictly speaking, Irwin was a hired hand, but Mam had taken him under her wing and treated him like a son. She'd bought him sturdy work boots, sewn him new shirts and pants and bought him a Delaware-style Amish straw hat. And when she realized how bad his eyesight was, she'd removed money from the crock in the root cellar and taken him to an optometrist. Now, Irwin sported new wire-frame glasses, was doing much better in his schoolwork and didn't peer down his nose like a weasel at everyone.

Miriam washed her hands, got a pitcher of water and another of milk from the refrigerator and brought them to the table. Eli was there, as usual, seated across from Ruth and staring at her as though she were the prettiest thing he'd ever seen in his life. Susanna took her seat, followed by Mam, Anna and Ruth. Miriam hastily poured drinks for everyone and sat beside Anna. Everyone bowed their heads for silent grace and then they began to eat. Miriam loved Mam's potato soup. She made it with lots of onions and celery. They'd grown a lot of celery in the garden this year and Mam always found ways to use the extra.

"Silas stopped by the school this afternoon," Mam said. "His oldest son is coming from Oregon to take over the farm. Silas and Susan plan to move into the *Grossdaadi* house."

"Eli's been hired to do some renovations to the place," Ruth explained. "Silas wants to close in the porch to make a room to fix clocks."

Anna nodded. "Silas's son and daughter-in-law have a big family."

"They do," Mam agreed. "Four younger ones will be coming to school, and I believe there are four older unmarried boys and a grown daughter."

"Four?" Susanna giggled as she buttered a biscuit. "That's good. Maybe one of them will want to marry Anna. Or me!"

"Hush, Susanna." Anna's face flushed. "What a thing to say."

"But you don't have a boyfriend." Susanna waved a dripping spoon. "Roofie has Eli. Miriam has Charley, and—"

"Charley is *not* my boyfriend," Miriam corrected.

Susanna bounced up and down in her chair. "But Anna said so! Anna said he was courting you." She turned to her sister. "Didn't you, Anna?"

"Shh, daughter." Mam passed the honey to Susanna. "Put some of this on your biscuit."

Susanna's round face screwed up. "But Anna did say Charley—"

At that instant, Miriam's pocket began to play a ringtone. Horrified, she snatched the phone out of her apron and fumbled with the buttons in an attempt to shut off the loud country tune. The cell phone slipped through her fingers, hit the floor and slid across the smooth linoleum, coming to rest under the table.

"What was that?" Susanna cried. "Is it a radio?" She peered under the table.

Eli tried to keep a straight face, failed miserably and began to choke into his napkin.

Miriam got down on her hands and knees and scrambled for the phone.

"It is!" Susanna declared, popping her head up over the edge of the table. "It's a radio!"

Miriam reached for the phone just as Irwin gave it a little kick, sending it spinning away to lodge under Anna's chair.

"Irwin!" Miriam squealed.

Irwin snickered. "Sorry." By now, Eli was roaring with laughter and Irwin's terrier was barking loudly and racing around the table.

Anna scooped up the phone, which had begun another round of music, and tossed it to Miriam who turned it off.

Miriam slowly climbed out from under the table, tucked the offending phone back into her apron pocket and took her seat. Anna clamped her hand over her mouth and made muffled noises of amusement. Ruth's lips were pressed tightly together, but she was trying so hard not to laugh out loud that tears were rolling down her cheeks. Eli gave up and fled to the porch, still laughing.

Mam, seemingly deaf and oblivious to the chaos in her kitchen, rose from her chair, went to the stove and filled her soup bowl a second time. "Would anyone like more soup?"

Miriam stared at her. It wasn't possible that Mam hadn't heard the phone ring. "Mam," she began softly. "I—"

"Miriam has a radio," Susanna said. "I want one, too. Can I have a radio, too?" When Susanna said it, it came out more *way-de-o* than *radio*, but everyone understood her perfectly.

"Eli," Mam called. "Would you like to come in off the porch and have more soup?"

He opened the kitchen door and came back in, still red-faced.

Irwin looked from Miriam to Mam and back to Miriam. "She has something in her pocket," he said.

Miriam glared at him.

"I would rather you don't bring your cell phone to family meals," Mam said, returning to the table with another bowl of the steaming soup. "It's not fair to interrupt the rest of us."

Miriam felt as though she was about to burst into tears, and they wouldn't be tears of laughter. "You're right. I'm sorry." She removed the phone from her pocket and held it out to her mother.

"I assume that John lent it to you so that you could... call him if Molly took a turn for the worse." The expression in Mam's gaze was loving and admonishing at the same time. She didn't take the phone. "It may be that there is some problem. Perhaps you should go outside and call him back."

She nodded, feeling like she did the day she'd pulled all the tail feathers out of Aunt Martha's peacock. She'd been ten years old then, but she could still remember this same look from her mother. "I didn't mean for it to disturb supper."

"I'm sure you didn't." Mam glanced around the table. "Who wants apple pie with vanilla ice cream for dessert?"

Miriam carried the cell phone back to the milk house, went inside and closed the door behind her. Her hands were shaking as she punched the button that dialed John.

He answered on the second ring. "Miriam?"

"*Ya.* It's me."

"I was wondering if you'd found a way to go with me tomorrow to Easton to pick up those supplies for the practice. I don't want to get you in trouble, but…but I really want you to come."

"I promised Mam I'd go to Johanna's tomorrow. To help her with the applesauce. I don't know how to get out of it." She wouldn't tell him about getting caught with the phone, at least not now she wouldn't. The fault was hers. How could she have been so foolish as to leave it turned on in her pocket? Now everyone in the family had had a laugh at her expense, Susanna would spread the news at church and there would be a price to pay later with Mam.

"I'm not leaving until eleven. I have to make two calls first in the morning. If you change your mind, you can reach me. How's Molly?"

"There's still a discharge from the hoof, but I'm cleaning it exactly like you showed me." Now that they were talking about the mare, Miriam felt more comfortable. She knew that she should hang up and return to the house to clean up the supper dishes, but it was nice sitting here in the semi-darkness chatting with John. She loved hearing the sound of his voice, and when he spoke, she could picture him as he'd been at lunch.

Would it be so terrible if she went with him in the truck tomorrow? She wasn't a child. She was a woman grown. Surely, she could ride in a friend's vehicle and have lunch at a restaurant without causing a scandal, couldn't she?

The following morning, Miriam sat across from Johanna at her kitchen table, explaining last night's disaster with the cell phone. Her sister had cut a generous slice of Mam's pie for each of them and had made a pot of herbal tea. Little Jonah was playing on the floor with a wooden top and the baby was asleep upstairs.

"I tell you, Mam didn't blink an eye," Miriam said.

"I wish I could have been there." Johanna chuckled. "I would have loved to see Susanna and that silly Eli."

"But I feel so bad."

"For what? Being young?" Johanna cut off a forkful of pie, bent and popped it into Jonah's mouth.

"More!" he cried.

"No more until after your lunch." Johanna wiped the corner of his mouth with her thumb. "Who didn't eat his cereal this morning?"

"I like pie."

"I'm sure you do. Now, be a good boy and run upstairs and see if Katie is still sleeping."

Obediently, Jonah scampered away to do as she'd asked. When he was safely out of hearing range, Johanna clasped Miriam's hand. "You're doing nothing wrong, sister," she said. "You're *rumspringa*."

"You know our church doesn't recognize *rumspringa*."

"Not *officially*, because they're concerned for our safety." Johanna gave her a sly smile. "But they recognize the *spirit* of it. Within limits. The point is that you're young and not yet baptized. You're supposed to jump the fence now and then."

"But with a Mennonite boy?" Miriam had already told Johanna about John, about how she felt about him and about the invitation to ride to Easton with him. The only thing she hadn't shared was what had happened with Charley and his friends at Spence's.

Johanna squeezed her hand. "The man you pick will be your husband for the rest of your life. Don't choose too hastily and don't close any doors."

"But if…" It was hard to talk about this, even with Johanna, because she didn't know herself what she wanted. "What if I don't know what I want? Who I want?

Everyone's trying to pair me up with Charley, but my heart tells me that John…" She let her sentence go unfinished; she didn't know quite what she was trying to say.

Johanna made a small sound of impatience. "You have to be careful with that. Your heart can play tricks on you. You've known Charley all your life. He's a good man, steady and he obviously cares for you. You can't ignore that."

"So you go along with Anna and Ruth? You think that—"

Johanna clapped her hands together once. "Hush. Listen to what I'm saying. No one can tell you who to love. How do you know what path God has chosen for you? Mam was born Mennonite. Is she a bad person?"

"No, but—"

"So. Mam is a good person and John is a good person. But you don't know if you're really attracted to *him* or to the fact that he's different than what you know. John's exciting. He makes your heart race and sends chills down your backbone."

A lump formed in Miriam's throat. "You're teasing me."

"No, I'm not. I'm telling you, don't be afraid to find out what you want. Go with John to Easton. So long as you don't lie to Mam if she asks you where you were today, you haven't done anything terrible."

"But she'll say 'no' if I ask."

"Would she?"

"Maybe I should have asked her."

"What do you want to do, Miriam?"

She looked up shyly at her sister. "I want to go—more than anything."

"Then go. Call him on your fancy red cell phone and

tell him you've changed your mind. Go and have a good time." She leaned forward, her elbows on the table. "So long as you don't do anything that would shame Mam or yourself, you have nothing to worry about."

Miriam felt the phone in her pocket. "He may have changed his mind. He may not want me to go now."

Johanna rose and went to a row of pegs on the wall and took down a blue scarf. "Of course, he does. Take this. If you wear my scarf, instead of your *kapp,* the English won't stare at you as they pass by in their vehicles."

"Take off my *kapp?*" Miriam's eyes widened. "What will John think?"

"He'll think you are a pretty girl that he likes having along for the ride. If he is the man you think he is, he will think nothing bad. But if he has other thoughts about one of Hannah Yoder's daughters, improper thoughts, best you learn that right away."

Chapter Eight

John took his eyes off the road long enough to glance at Miriam, sitting beside him in the cab of the truck. "You're not sorry you changed your mind and came along, are you?" he asked her.

She looked up from the radio dial she'd been adjusting, and the expression in her cinnamon-brown eyes answered his question. *"Ne."* She shook her head. "I'm not. Are you sorry you asked me?"

"No way, this has been fun. Really. I'm so glad that you took me up on it."

He couldn't get over how different she looked without her *kapp.* The blue checked headscarf covered only the crown of her head and the bun at the nape of her neck. He hadn't realized how pretty her auburn curls were in the sunlight or how easily she'd been able to slip into his world. He'd expected Miriam to be uncharacteristically quiet—even shy, out of her element—but she wasn't. She'd taken the restaurant in stride, just as she had the unexpected stop to assist an injured cat they found in the road.

They'd come upon the Siamese cat, lying in the other lane, soon after they'd crossed the Delaware-Maryland line on the way to Easton. Miriam had been out of the truck before he'd even turned off the engine. The animal was bleeding from the mouth and he assumed that a vehicle had hit it. Ignoring his warning to be careful, she'd snatched up a towel from the back of the truck, dashed out into the road and scooped up the cat before an approaching tractor trailer could finish it off.

His method would have been more cautious. He wouldn't have moved the animal until he'd assessed the damages it had suffered and made sure it wouldn't bite him, but Miriam hadn't hesitated. "He's not seriously hurt," she had pronounced, murmuring soothing sounds to the cat as she approached his truck. "He just had the wits knocked out of him. I think he's lost a tooth."

A little water applied to the scrapes and a few moments' time proved Miriam's diagnosis to be top-notch. Within minutes, a woman had come out of a nearby house, claimed the cat and she'd promised to take it to her own vet for a thorough checkup. But since the cat was squalling so indignantly and squirming so strongly, John had to agree with Miriam. The cat may have used up one of its proverbial nine lives, but it seemed fine.

"How did you know that it wasn't hurt badly?" he'd asked Miriam at lunch, over a crab cake sandwich, coleslaw and French fries.

She'd shrugged. "I just knew. Don't you feel it when animals are sick or dying? When you look into their eyes, you can tell."

"Not very scientific."

"Ne." She'd grinned at him. "But there's more to caring for animals than the science of it, isn't there?"

"Are you ever wrong?" he'd asked.

"Only our Lord was perfect. I make mistakes every

day." She'd wrinkled her nose mischievously. "I just try not to make the same ones over and over."

Her mention of God had made him a little uneasy. He'd been raised in a Mennonite home, and his mother and sister were active in the church. As a boy, he'd attended the youth functions and never missed services, but he didn't consider himself particularly religious.

"I think you have a gift," he'd said. "Uncle Albert has it. I've seen him treat animals that I've thought would be fine. He believed that they'd die and they did. And I've watched him deliver a seemingly dead calf and bring it back to life."

"Not him," she'd corrected softly. "He may have helped, but it is the Almighty that gives life and takes it away."

"Maybe. Or maybe the God you have such faith in touches some people, giving them knowledge they wouldn't otherwise have."

She'd shrugged again. "We all do our best, John. But we can't save them all. Some animals have a will to live and get better and some give up. I believe Molly's hoof will heal. Don't you?"

He'd been reluctant to answer. The mare's infection was proving difficult and he'd already decided that he'd ask Uncle Albert to come with him when he made his next visit to the Yoder farm. He hoped his uncle would have some idea as to what to do next, because he knew how much the horse meant to Miriam and her family.

"What would your mother say if she knew you were seeing an Amish girl?" she'd asked, changing the subject and surprising him with her candidness.

He'd chuckled. "Am I *seeing* an Amish girl? Is this what this is? Or is it two colleagues spending an afternoon together?"

"I'll have to think about that," she'd replied as she stole one of his fries, dipped it in ketchup and ate it.

"What about you? Will you be in trouble? If you're seeing an Englisher?"

"You're not English, you're Mennonite."

"Okay. Will you be in trouble if you're dating a Mennonite?"

Miriam had nodded solemnly and then smiled. "Absolutely. But this is my *rumspringa* time. I've got an excuse."

"*Rumspringa,* hmm?"

"*Ya.* Don't you watch television? Some Amish throw off their *kapps* and run wild."

He'd laughed. "So I've heard." And then he'd leaned closer. "Seriously, you should think about what I said. You have a gift for healing. Have you ever thought of going to veterinary school yourself?"

"Thought of it, but it's impossible," she'd replied. "So long as I remain in the community, my education is finished. My church doesn't believe in an English education. We are Plain people."

He'd wanted to take her hand, but sensed that if he did, she'd retreat from him. Instead, he met her gaze. "But you're different than the others, Miriam. You don't seem to be the kind of person to live your life behind walls."

"Walls to some, maybe," she'd agreed. "Loving arms to others."

"I'd like you to meet my sister sometime. I think you'd like her."

"Is she at home with your mother?"

"No. She's away at school. She's a college sophomore and she's studying to be an elementary teacher."

Miriam had nodded. "I thought about taking the teaching job at Seven Poplars School, when Mam remarries. I think I'd like it, being with the children every day."

"Hannah's getting married?"

She'd shrugged. "It's been two years since Dat died. She'll be expected to take a new husband soon. It's our way."

"And the lucky man?"

She'd then smiled mischievously. "I think it will be Samuel Mast. He's younger than Mam, but he spends a lot of time with his feet under our table. He has five children who need a mother, but he's well set up. His farm is one of the finest in the county. As Anna would say, Samuel is a catch."

"What makes you think it's your mother who attracts him? It might be you he likes."

"Me?" She'd chuckled at the idea. "*Ne.* Not me. Samuel likes women who are more...*meadle.*" She'd used her fingers to tug the corners of her mouth into the caricature of a smile. "A girly-girl. Not so tomboy as me. Samuel would be ashamed to see his wife behind a plow or mending a fence."

"Don't sell yourself short, Miriam," he'd said. "You're special. And if Samuel Mast or any other man can't see that, then he doesn't deserve you."

"And what makes you think I'd want Samuel? Or *any* husband for that matter?"

He'd thrown up his hands in surrender. "I stand corrected." And they'd both laughed easily together.

A few moments later, he'd ordered them each a refill of their sodas to go, and reluctantly, he'd turned toward Kent County and home. She'd remained in the truck, listening to the radio, when he stopped at an Easton veterinary practice and picked up several nineteenth-century veterinary surgical tools that Dr. Bierhorst, who was retiring, was giving to his grandfather. They'd then laughed and talked easily the rest of the way to Seven Poplars.

"Where do you want to get out?" he asked her as he approached the Amish schoolhouse. It was after four, the children had all left and her mother would probably be home at the farmhouse. "Should I take you back to your sister's?"

"Ne." She lifted her chin.

Sunlight, coming through the window, tinted the freckles on her nose the color of gold dust, and he felt a rush of protectiveness. "Where, then?" He didn't want her in trouble for going with him. The truth was, there would be consequences for them both once others found out. *If* others found out.

Neither mother, he suspected, would be happy. His mother would probably be the more upset of the two. His mother held certain beliefs about the Old Order Amish; she thought they were backward and uneducated. He had to agree with her that they were uneducated, he supposed, but many were every bit as intelligent as students that he'd worked with in college. And, as farmers or craftsmen, few could surpass them. He'd always admired the strong work ethic among the Plain people— he'd just never thought that he would be so attracted to a young woman whose background and faith were so different from his own.

"Take me home," Miriam said.

He blinked. "Home?"

"Ya, John."

He liked the way she said his name, the same as everyone else, but different—solid. He smiled at her. "You're brave."

She laughed. "In for a penny, in for a pound." And

then her gaze grew pensive. "I went with you and I had a good time. I won't ruin that by lying to my mother."

"Sure, I'll take you home, if that's what you want. But if she doesn't ask where you were—"

She leaned close and brushed his lips with the tips of two fingers. She smelled of green apple shampoo and something elusive, something fresh and sweet, something that brought a constriction to his throat.

"Hush, don't say it. Don't tempt me, John. Believe me, with Mam, it's better to come clean and face whatever storm comes."

Her fingers were warm and her touch was almost a caress. "If your mother is angry with you, Miriam, I should go in with you."

Miriam shook her head. "Tomorrow will be soon enough for that. I know her better than you. Today, she will not want to deal with you. She'll tell me what she thinks and she'll pray tonight. I have no doubt that she'll have plenty of fuss left over for you in the morning.... If you happened to come by to check on Molly."

"If you think that's best. But I feel like a coward."

Miriam chuckled. "Sometimes even the most courageous of men must be diplomatic. If Mam loses her temper with me, we'll hug and make up, but if she loses it with you and says things she later regrets, she will be shamed. You're not one of us, John, and you don't understand our ways. For Mam's sake, wait. I promise you, she may yet burn your ears tomorrow."

Mam was standing on the back porch, arms folded over her chest, watching as John stopped the truck. Miriam could feel her mother's gaze on her as she got out. "See you tomorrow," she called.

"First thing in the morning." John waved at her mother and pulled away. "Hannah."

"So, he drove you home from Johanna's," Mam said as Miriam approached the steps.

Miriam steeled herself. "No. He asked me to ride to Easton and have lunch with him and I did."

"You told me you were going to your sister's."

"*Ya,* Mam. I did, but then I went with John."

Her mother stepped in front of her, blocking her path. "John Hartman is not Amish."

"I know that, Mam."

"Hmm."

A flicker of something that might have been respect flickered in her mother's eyes. Miriam took a deep breath. "I rode in John's truck and ate lunch in a restaurant in the middle of the day. I did nothing to be ashamed of. You have my word."

"So, my daughter comes and goes as she pleases without a word to me?"

Miriam touched her arm. "I have to see for myself, to know which path God wants me to take."

Mam nodded. "So I told your uncle. Reuben saw you in John's truck and came here after school to tell me. He asked me if I knew what you were doing."

Miriam swallowed. "What did you tell him?"

Hannah folded her arms over her chest. "I said that he should take care of his daughter and leave you to me and your sisters."

Miriam's eyes widened. "You didn't!"

"*Ya,* she did." Anna pushed open the screen door and stepped onto the porch. "You should have seen the look on Uncle Reuben's face."

"He wasn't happy," Ruth called over Anna's shoulder. "A fine mess you've made, Miriam. Today, of all days."

Miriam glanced back at her mother. "Why? What's wrong? Is someone sick?"

"We are all well, except for Rebecca," Mam said. "I had a phone call at the chair shop today from Rebecca. Eli had to fetch me from the school. *Grossmama* has had a bad week. She tried to push Ida down the stairs and she gave Rebecca a black eye."

"*Grossmama* hit her? Poor Rebecca!" Miriam said.

"Ida thinks her mother and Jezebel and your sisters should come here now, instead of waiting for Ruth's wedding," Mam said going back up the steps to the porch. "I agree. Your grandmother is too much for Leah and Rebecca right now. I told them to arrange for a driver and I would pay the cost."

"I'm so glad," Miriam cried, following her. "I've missed Leah and Rebecca so much."

"We've been cleaning," Anna said. "Getting the bedrooms ready for *Grossmama* and Great Aunt Jezebel."

"When are they coming?" Miriam asked.

"As soon as Leah can hire a van," Mam said. "I should have insisted they come home before this. It was too much on your sisters."

Miriam took her mother's hand and they followed Anna and Ruth into the kitchen. "Will they be here before the house-raising on Saturday?"

Mam shrugged. "Who can say? But we have more than enough to keep us busy. Your *Grossmama* was never easy, and she will be even more difficult, now that she's not herself."

"And she hates us," Susanna piped up from where she stood near the stove. She'd obviously been baking because there were sugar cookies cooling on the table, and she had flour all over her apron and on her nose.

"Not hate," Mam corrected. "That is not a word we use, Susanna. We hate no one."

"Bad people?" Susanna suggested.

"*Ne*. We hate no one," Mam repeated firmly. "I'm sorry to say that I'm not her favorite person, but I don't believe that *Grossmama* hates me."

"So why can't Aunt Martha take her?" Miriam asked. "*She's* her daughter."

"Because *Grossmama* dislikes Aunt Martha even more than she does Mam," Ruth said, a smile tugging at the corners of her mouth.

Mam put an arm around Miriam's shoulder. "Enough of such talk, girls. Your Aunt Martha has her own burdens to bear. Imagine what living in this house would be like if we could not have peace in our own kitchen? If a mother and daughter were constantly at odds? You should find charity in your hearts for your aunt, not criticize her."

"Aunt Martha is too much like *Grossmama*," Anna mused.

"That may be," Mam said, "for people sometimes suggest that my daughters are as wayward as I was."

"You, wayward? Never." Miriam pinched a broken piece of cookie from the table and popped it in her mouth.

"In any case, your grandmother, her sister Jezebel, and Leah and Rebecca will be here in a matter of days," Mam said, "and we must be ready to welcome them."

"On top of the house-raising," Ruth reminded.

"So…" Mam's eyes narrowed. "Miriam. Where is your *kapp?* Don't tell me you went among the English with your head covered only by a scarf?"

"I thought it would cause less talk."

"A scarf is a head covering," Anna put in hopefully. She was a good sister, always there to defend Miriam.

"But not Plain enough when among the English. Next time, you will wear your *kapp* or not go into a restaurant at all." Mam arched an eyebrow. "Unless you're ashamed of us."

"Ne," Miriam said. "I'm not ashamed of my faith."

"Praise God for that, at least." Her mother turned away. "Go on, now, and help your sisters with the up-stairs floors. I'll cook supper."

"But the chickens need—"

"Irwin is tending the animals. You need not concern yourself until milking time. And one more thing." Her mother turned back, both hands resting on her hips.

"Ya?"

"You had a visitor this afternoon. Just before Uncle Reuben arrived."

"Who?" Miriam asked.

"Charley. He wanted to talk to you. He says he's been trying all week."

Miriam's heart sank. "Charley Byler?"

Anna snickered. "And what other Charley has been mooning around our back door like a lovesick calf?"

"He tells me he has promise of steady work," Mam said. "And he asked my permission to court you."

Chapter Nine

By eight on Saturday morning, the sound of hammers and saws echoed across the Yoder farm. The day was bright, the grass still damp with dew and the air redolent with the first hint of autumn. Next to Hannah's house, women and girls set up tables in the yard, while boys took charge of arriving horses and buggies. At the construction site across the field, six men were already raising the frame of the first wall on Ruth's new home. Friends and neighbors were coming from every direction, on foot, in wagons piled high with lumber and on push-scooters.

At the site of the new house, Miriam, Ruth and Anna walked among the newcomers, offering mugs of steaming coffee, paper cups of apple cider and apple donuts dusted with sugar that Anna had just pulled from the oven. Ruth's cheeks glowed pink with excitement as she tossed a hot donut to Eli.

"Who made this?" he asked with a grin. "You or Anna?"

"Eat it and guess," Ruth replied.

He propped his hammer against the foundation, took

a bite of the cake and teasingly held it out to her. "Good. Really good. Must be Anna's."

Giggling, Ruth snatched the donut and ran off to finish it, while Eli mimed his loss to his laughing companions.

As a wedding gift, Mam had given Ruth thirty acres of land with fine road frontage, across from the chair shop where Eli worked. Unsaid, but understood, was that if he worked hard, Eli would someday become a partner with Roman in the business that Dat had started years ago.

No wonder Ruth was so happy; she had a good man who loved her and her friends and neighbors were building them a new house and barn. And perhaps, best of all, she'd never have to be far away from Mam and Susanna and Johanna. She'd always have the blessings of church and family close around her.

Anna, on the other hand, seemed a little wistful to Miriam this morning. Anna would never envy a spoonful of joy of her sisters', but it had to hurt that at twenty-one, no one had ever asked to drive her home from a singing or chose her picnic basket at a school auction. No boy had ever come courting Anna and none had tried to steal a kiss behind the schoolhouse. What Anna had said was true. It wasn't fair that Miriam had two fellows wanting to walk out with her while Anna had none.

Please, God, Miriam prayed silently. *Can't You send someone who doesn't care that my sister is so Plain? Someone who can see past her big hands and broad shoulders to the beauty inside?*

"Anna!" a male voice called.

Miriam turned hopefully to see who was calling her sister's name, but her heart sank when she saw that it was only Samuel, wanting coffee and a donut. Why couldn't it have been Roland or Titus seeking her out, or even one of the boys from the other Amish churches?

"Good donuts," Samuel said, reaching for a second. "You make the best apple donuts, Anna."

Peter and Rudy ran up, and each waited for a donut. If Samuel wasn't there, they would have begged Anna and she would have given them one, no matter how many they'd already had, but they had a healthy respect for their father. The two were mischievous, but they usually pulled their pranks out of Samuel's sight.

Anna took pity on them and handed each one a donut. "Are you boys helping with the building?"

"*Ne,*" Samuel said, removing his hat and wiping the sweat off his forehead. "These rascals would be more in the way than they're worth. Back to Hannah's with the two of you," he ordered. "Tend to the horses and do whatever the women ask."

"Daa-t," Rudy whined. "Can't we—"

"Off with you."

Peter looked at Anna, hoping for support, but she shrugged and the two dashed off toward the big house.

"Good coffee, too," Samuel told Anna, holding up his mug. "Strong, like I like it."

"Samuel!" Roman called. "We need you on this beam."

Samuel lingered for a moment. "Well, duty calls." He nodded to Miriam and Anna and strode back toward the spot where the men waited to raise another wall.

Anna watched him walk away, a big man, tall and broad, nearing forty, and in the prime of his strength. "He'll make a good stepfather," she said. "He'll provide well for Mam and Susanna."

Miriam nodded. The thought of her mother remarrying was beginning to become more acceptable. No one would ever take the place of Dat. No one could. But Samuel would be kind to Susanna and Mam would have the little boys she'd always wanted. Peter and Rudy needed a mother, as did their younger sisters. It would be a sensible match, with the two farms running side by side.

"I'll have some of that cider."

Anna poked Miriam. "You awake?"

Miriam realized that someone had been speaking to her. She'd been so lost in her thoughts that she hadn't noticed. She turned and nearly bumped into Charley.

"I thought I'd best get some of those donuts before Samuel and his twins ate them all," he said.

"Help yourself," she said, giving him her full attention.

He took a mug of cider from her tray. "Good day for a house-raising."

She nodded. It was a good day and she was grateful to God for the kind weather. A hard rain would have delayed the construction, but this day was perfect, not too hot, with a light breeze. "The house will be perfect for them. You did a fine job on the foundation, Charley. I know Ruth and Eli are grateful for your hard work."

A slow smile spread across his face. He *was* a nice-looking boy, with an honest chin and warm eyes. "I try my best," he said.

She nodded. "I mean it. Everyone knows how solid your work is. You deserve the new position helping build the new wing at the hospital."

Anna moved away, leaving them in what would be the barnyard of the new place. The grass here was nearly knee-high in places, and the last of the Queen Anne's lace and black-eyed Susans lingered, adding their white and gold and brown to the green carpet that spread out around them. Usually, the cows pastured here, but Mam had kept them out of the field for the last two months, due to the construction. Eli would probably get a good hay crop off his acres before winter.

"Oops." Charley laughed as a honeybee landed on the rim of his cup. "Wouldn't want to swallow that."

"Your cider would have a kick," she agreed, with a chuckle.

"Ya." He nodded and took a sip of cider. "Heard your grandmother isn't coming, after all. That's too bad. I know Leah and Rebecca would have liked to have been here for this."

"All the arrangements were made, then *Grossmama* fell again. The same hip. The doctor says she can't travel for now." She met Charley's gaze, knowing he would understand how her heart went out to her sisters. "Poor Leah and Rebecca, they're having a time. But both refused to come home when Mam offered to try to make other arrangements."

"Your sisters are nice girls. Of course, I think all the Yoder girls are." He cut his eyes at her.

Miriam smiled at him. She just couldn't help herself. Charley always made her feel good about herself. "You should go back to work."

"I should. But listen, I need you to do something for me. I want you to send Irwin with the refreshments," Charley said. "Later, when all the men get here. The talk might get a little rough." He grimaced. "Not for your ears."

"I'll keep that in mind." She didn't know that she agreed with him necessarily, but she appreciated his thoughtfulness.

"Men tell jokes. Sometimes they are not...what you

would hear at church." He glanced at his feet. "No harm is meant, but…"

She touched his sleeve. "It's okay. I understand."

"Good." He looked up. "You and Anna, any of you, shouldn't hear such things."

"And women talk about matters men certainly don't want to hear," she told him. "So we're even."

"We're even." He nodded with a smile.

"Now, I'll ask something of you, Charley," Miriam said. "Be pleasant to John, if he comes."

"What? You think he might not show?"

"I don't know if he will or not. He might be called out on a case. But if you're mean to him, I'll be very unhappy. It wouldn't be fair. Most of the people here are Amish. He might feel like an outsider."

"He *is* an outsider, Miriam. That's the thing. He's a nice guy. I like John, but he isn't one of us." He looked right into her eyes. "And he isn't for you."

She stiffened. "That's for *me* to say, not you."

"Miriam! I'm going back to the house for more coffee and donuts," Anna called. "That second batch should be out by now."

She shoved the tray of cider into Charley's hands. "Wait! I'll come with you!"

"*Dangi,*" Charley called after her. "For the cider."

"Just remember what I said about John. Don't be rude to him."

"Wouldn't think of it."

As Miriam and Anna walked away, Anna leaned close and whispered. "You're too hard on him."

Miriam sighed. "You're probably right. It's just that I don't know what to do about him. For years, he was content to be the boy I'd play in the mud with. Now, he wants more of me, and I…I don't know if I can give that."

"Well, just be sure that's really how you feel," Anna said. "Some other girl will snatch him up and you may be sorry." She took Miriam's hand. "Like what happened to Johanna's Roland."

"Johanna's Roland?" Miriam stared at her in surprise. "I know they used to walk out together, but that was before she met Wilmer. She's a married woman. You shouldn't say such things about our sister. That's all in the past."

"Mmm," Anna replied. "*Ya,* it is in the past, but it's still what happened. If Johanna and Roland hadn't argued, he might be our brother-in-law instead of Wilmer. And I think Johanna would be a lot happier." She whispered the last sentence in Miriam's ear.

Miriam stopped and looked into Anna's eyes. "Do you know something I don't? Has Johanna complained about her husband?" she asked, in shock.

Anna shook her head. "*Ne.* Johanna would never complain, but I watch her. I see her look at Roland sometimes, when she thinks no one is watching. Her heart is heavy, twin."

Miriam thought about what Anna was saying. "I've never really liked Wilmer, but he's a devoted church member and he provides well for his family. What do you think is wrong? What have I missed?"

"Sometimes I don't think you notice what's in front of your nose."

"What haven't I noticed?" Miriam asked, feeling badly that she hasn't been more aware of what was going on in her dear sister's life.

Anna bent and picked a black-eyed Susan. For a few seconds, she twirled it between her big, plump fingers and then began to pluck the petals, one at a time. "It is wrong to bear false witness and wrong to gossip, but my heart aches for Johanna, so to you, I will confide what I suspect."

Miriam waited, her breath caught in her throat.

"Do you see Wilmer playing with Jonah?"

"*Ne.* I never have, but I thought that maybe when he was older…" She trailed off. "Not all men are like Samuel or our Dat. Many don't have an easy way with young ones."

"Wilmer is dark—dark beard, dark bushy eyebrows, swarthy skin. Roland is fair, as is little Jonah."

"What of it? Johanna is a redhead like the rest of us. It's only natural that Jonah be fair-skinned with light hair. He takes after our family."

"And the baby, Katie? She is dark-haired like Wilmer, *ne?*"

Miriam took a step back. "Stop it, Anna. That's evil. You're not suggesting that Wilmer isn't Jonah's father, are you?"

Anna's eyes grew hard as winter wheat. "I would never suggest such a terrible thing. You know our Johanna. Pure she was on her wedding night. Mam and I washed her sheets. I saw the proof with my own eyes."

"Then why would you think such a thing?" Miriam shook her head. She'd never expected to hear such words out of Anna's mouth—not Anna. She thought well of everyone.

"I'm afraid Wilmer thinks otherwise," Anna confessed. "When Jonah was born, he took one look at him and walked out of the house. He didn't speak to Johanna until the following day, and I heard her tell Mam that Wilmer asked whose child he was."

"Such wickedness. He's a stupid man. Too foolish to realize what a good wife he has. But that was more than three years ago, nearly four. Surely, he can't…"

Anna shrugged. "All I know is that last year, when things seemed really bad between them, I saw Johanna with a bruise on her face. She said that she'd bumped into a pantry door, but there were also bruises that looked like fingerprints on her wrist. Mam went to Bishop Atlee. I don't think Wilmer has struck her again, but something is wrong in that house."

"And you never told me?"

"It was a great weight on my heart." She plucked the last petal from the black-eyed Susan and tossed the broken flower away. "Why should I burden you when I could pray for them myself? And I do, every night."

"Then why tell me now?"

Anna was thoughtful for a moment. "Because I think Johanna chose the wrong man. And I want to make sure that you, my dear twin, don't make the same mistake. You and I are almost the same person, despite our outward differences. Better for you to be an old maid like me than to make a bad marriage and live to regret it."

Miriam's knees went weak. How could this all have happened without her knowledge? And how could Anna have borne this trouble alone? "You think I mean to choose John? And leave the faith?"

"I believe John is a good person. I can't say what life God intends for you. Just be certain it's not the world that calls to you, rather than the man. You are wise in so many ways, much smarter than I am. But when it comes to simple truths, you sometimes rush past without seeing what is in front of you."

Miriam looked away. "You mean Charley. You think I'm discounting him?"

"I mean you must think about what is best for you. Not for the family. Not even for the church. Ask the Lord for guidance. Whatever you choose, this man or that, or none, I will always love you, Miriam. And I will always be there for you."

"Don't be so quick to judge yourself, Anna, or to say that you aren't smart. That's not true."

Anna sighed. "Which of us sat through third grade classes for two years, and which twin skipped the fifth grade?" Tears welled in her dark brown eyes. "It doesn't matter that I'm not a person for books. I bake the best apple donuts in the county, don't I?"

"In the country. No one in Ohio or Pennsylvania can touch you."

Her sister's eyes lit up with a smile. "Don't say such things. Would you have me guilty of *hochmut?*"

Miriam chuckled and they started to walk again. "A little of my own *hochmut* wouldn't hurt you. I have more than enough to share."

Anna's expression grew serious. "I do worry about my pride in my cooking. The Bible tells us that it is a bad thing."

"But honesty is right and good. And didn't Jesus tell us that we must love ourselves? You're a treasure. We all know it and you should, too."

"If only some young man would see it."

"Someone will," Miriam promised, grabbing her hand and squeezing it.

"That's what Mam says, but…" She sighed.

"No buts, twin. Who knows what could happen? You may marry before me. I think I like *rumspringa*. I may decide to stay single for years."

"Not too many, I hope. Your children will be as dear to my heart as the ones I will never mother. Unless some widower with eleven children takes pity on me." Anna giggled. "Not that I would mind stepchildren, but I look at Johanna's baby and I long for one of my own."

"All in His time." The beep of a horn behind her caught Miriam's attention and she turned and looked over her shoulder. John had just pulled into the yard beside the foundation of the new house. Behind his truck was a trailer piled high with a bathtub, sink and toilet. "Look!" Miriam pointed, turning back toward the new house. "John did come. What's all that stuff?"

"I don't know," Anna said. "But I'd guess it's a bathroom for Ruth and Eli. Let's go back and see."

"Charley won't like it," Miriam said. "Didn't he tell us to stay away from the work site?"

"*Ya,*" Anna agreed. "But you had no intention of doing so, did you?"

Miriam laughed. "*Ne.*"

"Nor me," Anna said, giggling. "Anybody who's been anywhere near Irwin when he's cleaning the pigpen would have heard those bad words already."

They strolled back across the field toward John's truck. He saw them coming and waved. Miriam stopped a few yards away, folded her arms over her chest and motioned to the trailer with her chin. "What's all that?"

John beamed. "For the house. One of Uncle Albert's clients is remodeling his house. They were going to throw everything in the dump. It's hardly been used at all. The tub and sink were from a guest bathroom. I hope they won't mind blue. For free?"

"Surely they should pay something," Miriam said. "They couldn't mean to give them away."

John shook his head. "Mr. O'Malley said Eli would be doing him a big favor if he took them off his hands. He'd have to pay to dispose of them and you pay by weight." The other men had stopped work and were walking toward the trailer. "Eli!" John called. "Take a look at this and see what you think."

Anna glanced at Miriam. "A whole bathroom! Lucky for Ruth and Eli."

"*Ya,*" Miriam agreed.

"These friends of John's are good people to share what they didn't need and John was good to think of it." Anna grimaced. "But what will Aunt Martha say if Ruth gets a *blue* toilet?"

Miriam laughed, putting her arm around her sister's waist. "The Lord *does* provide. And who are we to show *hochmut* and be too proud to use an Englishman's john?"

Chapter Ten

Charley knew he was in trouble when he saw John pull a tool belt from the bed of his pickup. He'd expected that John would bring a new hammer with the price tag still on it and little else. Instead, the wide leather belt that the Mennonite strapped around his waist was obviously well-used and of professional quality. Either John had borrowed an experienced carpenter's tools, or he had more experience than hammering just a few nails.

The day just seemed to get worse from there.

It wasn't long before John proved his worth in the construction, and Charley felt himself hard put to keep up with him. John not only knew the trade, but he was a hard worker who didn't mind taking orders from their gang boss. Charley's only saving grace was that while John might have been even more skilled with a hammer, Charley was definitely stronger, and was called upon several times when there was a heavy job to be done. Charley was ashamed that he'd misjudged the vet so quickly when he obviously hadn't known anything about him.

Charley didn't usually draw conclusions about people without careful consideration, but he felt a natural competition with John from the first day they'd met, when

Miriam had been all smiles introducing them. The thing was, he genuinely liked John. It was just that he felt threatened by John's obvious interest in Miriam.

An hour after John arrived, his uncle Albert and three other Mennonite boys showed up, ready to pitch in. "Sorry to come late," Albert said after he'd introduced his team. "I had an emergency at the office this morning."

"Glad to have you," Eli said. "The more hands, the quicker the work goes." Eli glanced at John. "He's no stranger to hard work."

Albert smiled and nodded. "He put himself through college working construction." Albert walked to the rear of his truck and fired up a gas-powered generator. In the bed of the truck were several different kinds of electric saws that could be run off the generator. "I thought we could set up a saw table."

"Sounds good to me," Eli shouted, above the roar of the motor. "Power saws will make the construction go even faster."

"Let's get this section up!" Samuel gave the signal, and the six men on his team, including John, began the strenuous task of raising the west wall of the house.

Charley threw his weight into the frame. The six of them lifted the heavy wooden structure into place, and Samuel and Eli began to attach braces. Charley pulled a handful of nails out of the bag on his belt and began hammering them in, securing the bottom wall plate to the floor joist. Beside him, John was doing the same thing. John's hammer struck with a steady rhythm and Charley quickened his pace to keep up.

Beside the house, Albert Hartman switched on a circular saw he'd plugged into his generator. Other men, Amish and Mennonite, carried lengths of marked lumber to be cut to size. From the other sides of the house, Charley could hear framing going up. Nearly thirty men had gathered to help with the house-raising, while another ten, under Johanna's husband's supervision, were working on Eli's new barn.

The more experienced men were detailed to the house site, while the boys and less-skilled carpenters built the stable and assembled a windmill. The barn had to be solid and waterproof, but the county inspector wouldn't be nearly as particular about that structure as he would the house. Neither would be wired for electricity; that went without saying.

By the time the dinner bell rang for the midday meal, Charley's shirt and hair were damp with sweat. His arms ached and his fingers had cramped from driving nails steadily for hours. John seemed equally ready for a break, but Charley watched to see that they laid down their hammers at the same time.

Unhooking their tool belts, they left them lying on the house's plywood subfloor and walked across the field toward Hannah's house and the waiting food. Neither Charley nor John spoke directly to each other, although there was plenty of easy talk and joking as the group of men prepared to fill their empty bellies and quench their thirsts.

When they reached the farmyard, men ahead of them had already lined up by the pitcher pump to wash their hands and faces. Charley motioned to John. "Over here," he said, leading the way to another faucet at the base of the Yoder's windmill. One of the girls had left a cake of soap and fresh towels.

John pulled off his ball cap, bent and stuck his head under the running water. His brown hair was cut short and he didn't seem to mind when his blue T-shirt took a fair share of wetting. Charley handed him a towel, and then began washing up.

Miriam came up behind them. "Food's on," she said. "Take a seat wherever you like at the tables."

Charley ran a hand through his wet hair, slicking it back off his face before putting his straw hat back on. Just looking at Miriam made his heart feel too big for his chest. He knew that a man wasn't supposed to dwell on outer appearances, that what was inside a person mattered more. But Miriam was so beautiful, like a butterfly in her lavender dress and starched white *kapp*.

He wanted to pull her into his arms and inhale the clean, sweet scent that was hers alone, but he knew better. If he tried to take advantage of their friendship, who could guess what she'd do? She'd certainly be angry. She'd push him away, maybe even shove him backward into the mud puddle and make a fool of him in front of John.

Charley knew he had no right to claim Miriam as his own; she'd given him no indication that she felt the same way about him. But every drop of blood in his body told him that this was the only woman for him. He might find someone else, marry her, make a family and live a Plain life, but he'd never feel the joy that burst inside him like Fourth of July firecrackers every time Miriam smiled at him.

He'd heard that she'd gone off with John in his truck without a chaperone. Everyone in the neighborhood had heard. Word was that Reuben had gone to the house to scold Hannah for letting Miriam run around with a Mennonite boy, but no more had come of it.

Most likely, Hannah had told her brother-in-law to mind her own business. Hannah was no shrinking violet.

She'd always stood up for her girls with all the pluck of a banty hen with a flock of chicks.

Miriam was like her mother Hannah in a lot of ways. She was strong. She'd make a good wife and a good mother. If he couldn't have her—if he lost her to John—he'd have to seriously consider leaving Kent County. He'd never be happy here, seeing her with another man, knowing they could never be together.

"Thanks for coming," Miriam was saying to John. "And tell your uncle and the others from your church how much we appreciate it."

John grinned.

Girls would think the Mennonite was decent-looking, Charley supposed. Not too old to marry for the first time, maybe twenty-nine or thirty. John's features were even and pleasant. He had good white teeth and eyes that met yours straight on when he spoke.

Charley didn't doubt that most girls would think John was a lot more handsome than he himself was. Charley didn't waste much time looking in a mirror, except to shave and he didn't grow a lot of beard to begin with. But he wasn't pie-faced or cross-eyed, at least, and he had a chin, not like his friend Menno whose jaw kind of melted into his neck.

Charley's eyes were a clear blue and his sandy hair was thick and a little unruly. He might not be as tall as John, but he had strong shoulders and good arms. He doubted that John could lift a three-month-old calf over his head without breathing hard...or guide a horse-drawn plow from sunup to sundown.

No, he was no Eli, who had a face that could sell toothpaste. He was just ordinary Charley. But his love for Miriam Yoder wasn't ordinary and he meant to marry her before the church and cherish her all the days of his life.

He'd not give her up without a fight and he'd be boiled for an egg if he'd let a Mennonite in a blue truck come between them.

All Charley had to do was convince *Miriam* that he was the man for her...

Somehow, Charley and John ended up sitting at the table, side by side. They had a place halfway down, right in their age group, between the young men, old enough to do a full day's work, and the married men. The older fellows, the preachers, Bishop Atlee, the deacons and John's uncle Albert were at a second table under the shade trees. The younger table was definitely the livelier of the two, with lots of laughter and joking. Charley always enjoyed this kind of fellowship with the men in his community, both married and unmarried. Days like this had a way of building bonds that would last a lifetime.

"More tea?"

Charley turned to see Miriam standing beside him, a brimming pitcher of iced tea in her hands. *"Dangi,"* he said. He offered his empty glass and Miriam filled it to overflowing. When a little spilled over, he set it down and licked his fingers.

"John? Would you like some?"

Charley was surprised when John said that he did. He'd hardly sipped his tea, and he hadn't eaten more than a little girl. He wondered if maybe Amish food didn't suit John. There was plenty to be had: every kind of meat, from baked ham to fried chicken, fried rabbit, hamburgers, hot dogs, turkey legs and platters of cold cuts. Bowls of macaroni salad, potato salad, three bean salad, Dutch slaw and cabbage-filled peppers were crowded beside tureens of hash browns and potato dumplings. Platters of deviled eggs, cheese, bread, celery and fried eggplant were surrounded by pickles, chowchow and vegetables of all kinds. There'd be more desserts than a sensible man could eat, but Charley didn't want to ruin his appetite until he'd finished the main courses. With all the work to be done this afternoon, he needed to keep up his strength.

"I can't believe how fast the house is going together," John said to Miriam.

"That's the idea. It's why so many people come together to help," she answered.

Charley didn't like the tone of her voice: soft, flirtatious. He could just see her out of the corner of his eye. Thinking fast, he drank his tea in three long gulps and held up his glass. "Miriam. I'd appreciate—"

"Maybe I should bring you a pitcher of your own," she teased, but she came back around him, away from John, and refilled the glass.

But John was sneaky. He tipped over his glass as pretty as could be, spilling tea on the tablecloth and on himself and Charley. "Oops. Miriam. I think I need a refill, too."

Charley wiped at his pant leg as the other guys at the table, knowing full well it hadn't been an accident, began to laugh. "Miriam, you'd better bring a barrel of tea for those two," Titus called.

"A wagon load," Menno chimed in.

Charley put his hand on the pitcher to keep her from returning to John. "What would you suggest for sweets?" he asked.

"Her!"

Whoever that wiseacre is will pay, Charley thought. "Mind your mouth," he snapped, throwing a warning glance in the direction of the guys seated across the table from him and John. "Miriam? Pie or cake? What looks best?"

"No dessert for you until you finish your dinner," she said. "John's plate is clean." She had an innocent expression on her face, but mischief twinkled in her eyes.

Charley knew that she was on to him when she pried his fingers off the iced tea pitcher.

She made a point of turning her attention to John, "John, would you like me to get you a clean glass?"

"I can get it, if you'll just show me the way." He was off the bench before she could answer and the other boys at the table hooted and stamped their feet. Before Charley could come up with anything equally clever to do, Miriam and John walked away, leaving Charley staring at a full glass of iced tea, two chicken legs and a mound of potato salad.

Anna, having witnessed the whole thing from the end of the table, walked over and leaned over Charley's shoulder. "Would you like to try some apple cider? Might have better luck."

He looked up to see her smiling at him and wiped at his wet pant leg that was now sticky. "I think I'm already all wet."

"Not to worry," she soothed, quietly, her words meant only for him. "Miriam's coming to the young people's singing tonight, and it's Amish only. John won't be invited. You'll have her all to yourself."

He nodded and reached for the piece of chicken on his plate. Maybe Miriam would let him drive her home from the gathering. When he got her alone, he could ask if he could court her. Now that he'd spoken with Hannah, he was free to do so. He doubted John had gotten *that* far, otherwise he'd have surely heard. Things might be dark, but he hadn't lost yet. He still had a chance to win her heart, and the singing would be the perfect place to begin.

"I think you spilled the tea on purpose," Miriam said, when she handed John a new glass. "That wasn't very kind."

"No," he agreed. "It wasn't, was it?" He grinned. "I don't think Charley likes me very much."

"That's not it." She hesitated, trying to figure out how to explain her situation with Charley to John. Then she just came out with it. "Charley wants to court me. He hasn't asked me yet, but only because he hasn't been able to catch me alone. He already spoke to Mam."

John's gaze grew serious. "What are you going to say?"

She shrugged. "I don't know. That's the problem." She pressed her lips together.

He nodded. "It's a big decision. You should keep in mind that you have, you know, other options."

She looked up at him. "Do I?"

"Miriam!" Ruth called from across the yard. "We need more tea at the bishop's table."

"Guess I'm keeping you from your work. I'll get their table."

John picked up a second pitcher and she was filled with a pleasant surprise. Dat had been a great man, but never, in her life, had she seen him tend to such a menial task. "That's women's work."

"With Gramps and Uncle Albert, I'm the serving boy. I'm good at this. Watch me." John winked at her and strode toward the seniors' table. Some of the older men rolled their eyes, but either John didn't notice, or didn't care. He started refilling glasses and taking orders like he'd been doing it all his life.

Maybe he had, she thought. What did she know about how Mennonites did things? Or the English? Maybe men outside the Amish community washed dishes at their wife's side and swept front porches after supper. She knew so little about the outer world, and she had to admit, she was curious.

Uncle Reuben said something to John and waved him to an empty seat beside him. John glanced up at her, nodded to Reuben and sat down, placing the now-empty pitcher on the table.

Johanna came up beside Miriam, watching her, watching John. "People are talking about you and John," she whispered. "Better be careful."

"They wouldn't be talking if Charley wasn't so silly. He made a scene and called attention to us."

"Right." Johanna chuckled. "Speaking of making a scene, have you seen our mother?" She gestured toward the back porch where Mam seemed deep in conversation with a man in a blue checked shirt. "John's Uncle Albert. Albert Hartman."

"He's our guest. She has to be nice to him."

"Nice or *nice?*" Johanna put a finger to her lips and snickered.

"What do you mean?"

"While you're busy flirting with Charley and John, Mam's not above a little flirting of her own."

"I was not flirting!" Miriam's mouth gaped. "And how can you say such a thing about Mam?"

Johanna chuckled. "Use your eyes." She motioned toward their mother and Albert Hartman. "You know, they were sweet on each other when they were young."

"She'd never consider a Mennonite. She might have

grown up Mennonite, but she's Amish now." She turned to her sister. "She would never—would she?"

"Maybe the two of you aren't as different as you think," Johanna said with a shrug. "Maybe Mam is using Albert to push Samuel into popping the question. After all, Samuel's been putting his feet under her table for more than a year without ever coming right out and asking her to marry him."

"Maybe," Miriam agreed. "Or maybe God's will is more mysterious than we can understand. Maybe He wants women to follow their hearts, not their heads, even if it means taking a road less traveled."

"Some of the boys want cider," Dorcas said, approaching the drink table and filling her pitcher. She glanced at Johanna. "Did you tell her?"

"Ya." Johanna folded her arms. "Like I told you, it's nothing. Charley was making a joke, is all. Just being Charley."

Dorcas drew herself up to her full height and dried her hands on a towel. "You poke fun at him and it's wrong," she said. "He's worth two of that Mennonite boy."

Miriam prayed for patience. Dorcas was Anna's best friend. "I haven't done anything wrong."

"Flirting, leading a good man on. You call that right?" Dorcas sniffed. "My mother saw you, and she'll go to Hannah. You don't set a good example for the younger girls—how to act. Maybe you should think more about the hereafter and joining church, than riding in pickup trucks and making a scandal."

"And maybe you should think more for yourself, Dorcas, and not parrot everything your Mam says." Johanna dumped a scoopful of ice into her cousin's tea pitcher. "You might get a boyfriend or two of your own if you laughed more and criticized less."

Two bright pink patches glowed on Dorcas's cheeks as she snatched up the pitcher and hurried away.

"That was harsh," Miriam murmured to her sister.

Johanna shrugged. "Harsh but true. She needs somebody to set her straight or she'll never find a husband. She acts like she's forty."

"She's right, though. Aunt Martha will blame Mam for what I did. She always does."

"Don't worry about Mam. She can handle Aunt Martha."

"You girls serving or gossiping?"

Miriam whirled around, surprised to find Charley standing so close behind her. She felt her face grow hot and hoped he hadn't overheard what she and Johanna had been saying to each other.

"What do you want now?" she demanded.

"More tea." He held out an empty glass.

Her eyes widened, and Johanna giggled.

Charley laughed and lowered his glass. "*Ne.* I'm teasing you. I've had more than enough." He looked down at his damp trousers. "I'm not sure whether I'm wearing more iced tea than I drank or not. I came over because I wanted to ask you to ride home from the singing with me tonight."

"I think I'd best find something to do…somewhere else," Johanna said, walking away.

"*Ne.*" Miriam grabbed her sister's arm.

"So, will you, Miriam? Will you ride home with me tonight?" Charley pressed.

"Say *ya, Miriam!*" yelled Menno and Titus and Roland and a half dozen more young men at the table, all together.

"You know you want to," Menno added.

"Charley Byler, you are the most, most—"

"Persistent," Johanna supplied, giggling.

"That isn't what I was going to say," Miriam answered. She could feel her temper rising. All the men were staring at her, even those at the bishop's table. In another minute, she was going to dump a bucket of ice over Charley's head.

Johanna saw the look on Miriam's face, sighed, then turned to Charley. "Go back to the table and have your pie," she told him. "She'll ride with you."

Miriam clasped her hands to her sides, curling her fingers into tight fists. She didn't like being put on the spot by Charley in front of people this way. And Johanna wasn't helping matters. "I won't," she protested.

"She will," Johanna corrected, giving Charley a friendly nudge and waving toward his table. "Go on, now, before you embarrass her even more."

Charley grinned. "Later, then. I've got lots to talk to you about, Miriam."

"And I've got lots to say to you, too," she promised, her tone not nearly as kindly as his. "I can't wait."

Chapter Eleven

It was after eleven that evening when the young people's social at Norman and Lydia's farm finally broke up. It had been a long day, but Miriam was not in the least tired. The youth gathering, with the usual singing and party games, had been more fun than she'd expected, and even though Johanna had trapped her into riding home in Charley's buggy, she wasn't dreading it like she thought she would.

The get-together had been larger than normal, as teens and young adults from the neighboring districts who'd come to help raise the house and barn had been invited. Ruth and Charley, both with good voices, had acted as song leaders, while Eli had directed the circle dances, cornhusking contest and apple dunking. Miriam's all-girl team was defeated in the cornhusking by the boys, amid a thunder of stamping feet and raucous cheers. However, Susanna upheld the family honor by plunging her head completely underwater and coming up with the first apple in her teeth. Her prize was a basket of pears and she was so excited she could hardly talk.

The young people's dancing-games weren't the same as English dances, but were more like old-fashioned folk dances. The participants held hands and skipped in a large circle, while others clapped and sang along. The fun came when the couple in the center locked arms and moved in the opposite direction until one of them returned to the circle and chose another to take his or her place. Girls sometimes danced with other girls, but boys never did.

When the person leaving the circle picked a new victim, they usually sought out someone who would cause the most laughter from the group or the one they suspected their old partner was sweet on. It was the game leader's job to see that the teasing never became mean and that everyone was eventually chosen, so that no one was left out.

Adult chaperones kept their distance, and if some boys held hands with their partners a little longer than was necessary, or if they were more than enthusiastic when it came to swinging a girl, the behavior was usually overlooked, so long as the participants remained in full view of the group and no kissing or inappropriate touching occurred. Any infraction and the guilty party would find themselves banned from future events and their parents visited by district elders.

All the same, it was at these frolics that romances often blossomed, and a girl who'd never looked at a certain boy twice might decide that there might be more to him than she'd supposed. It was all very confusing to Miriam. She liked John, perhaps even wanted him to walk out with her, but watching Charley tonight made her less sure. He wasn't exciting and he didn't make her heart race…or did he?

Things had begun to look differently to Miriam when she'd accidentally overheard a conversation between Charley and John just after the men had finished the day's work on the new house. She'd finished the evening milking and had been about to leave the barn when she'd heard Charley, on the other side of the door, call John's name. When John murmured a response, she'd stopped short, hoping that Charley wouldn't cause trouble again.

"You did a good day's work for a college boy," Charley had said heartily.

She'd crept forward and peeked around the corner of the barn. John and Charley were standing in a group of men that included Roland and Samuel. Charley was grinning.

"And not just a good day's work for a Mennonite, either. A good day's work for an Amish," Charley had said as he extended his hand. "Sorry if I was a jerk before. Thanks for pitching in."

John had grasped the offered hand and shook it. "No problem. I was glad to be a part of it." He smiled. "I mean that. It was something, building a house that fast."

"We couldn't have finished as much as we did today without your help," Charley said. "You're all right for a Mennonite." The other men had laughed and John and Charley had both joined in.

Miriam had then retraced her steps to the cows, waited a few moments and then left the barn. By that time, the others had scattered. Neither John nor Charley were anywhere to be seen.

But Miriam hadn't been able to forget the conversation she'd overheard. Charley was obviously jealous of John, but he'd been man enough to admit when he was wrong and offer the hand of friendship. And he'd done it in front of his friends and neighbors. That took courage and reinforced what she already knew about her old friend. Charley had a good heart and he could laugh at his own mistakes. Realizing how important that was, somehow made her feel differently about him tonight. She hadn't been able to stop thinking about him. And when it had been Charley's turn to swing her around in *Skip to My Lou*, she'd found that his strong arm and the gleam in his eyes had sent goose bumps down her spine.

"Miriam?" Susanna's voice broke into Miriam's thoughts. "Help me." Panting, Susanna staggered out of the shadows, a heaping basket of pears in her arms. "They're falling everywhere."

The pears were piled high, and every time Susanna took two steps, one would roll off the top and fall to the ground. Then, her little sister would place the basket on the ground, put the errant pear back on, and pick up the container. It was far too heavy for Susanna to begin with, and there was no way she could maintain her balance long enough to reach the buggy without having the same thing happen over and over.

"Wait." Miriam scooped up another pear rolling through the grass.

Susanna trudged forward, mouth set, small rounded shoulders straining. "Did you see? Did you see me? I won! I dunked bester than anybody."

"You did dunk better than anyone else." Miriam took the basket from her sister's hands. "You were the best apple dunker of all. Wait until Mam hears."

"Can I have a pear?" Charley came out of the shadows and lifted the basket out of Miriam's grasp.

Susanna giggled. "*Ne.* Silly. They're green. Pears gotta wi-pen."

"Ripen," Miriam corrected softly. "And you're right, Susanna. They do have to ripen before we eat them."

Charley smelled good. Miriam caught the distinct scent of Old Spice aftershave as she leaned down to grab another pear Susanna had lost. She passed it to her sister. "Would you like to ride home with me in Charley's buggy?" she asked.

"Sorry, no room tonight." Charley placed Susanna's basket in the back of the Yoder buggy. Then he caught Miriam's hand. "Susanna will have to ride with Anna. I borrowed Roland's two-seater."

"Miriam," Anna said, already seated on the buggy bench. "Maybe you'd better not. Mam will say you should have a chaperone."

But Miriam let Charley lead her away by the hand and together they climbed into the courting buggy. Before she could think twice, Charley had gathered the lines and snapped them over the back of his pinto gelding. They rolled out of the farmyard with the horse at a fast trot.

"Miriam!" Anna called after them.

"See you at home!" she shouted back.

When they reached the end of the Beachy's lane, Charley turned the pinto's head in the opposite direction of the Yoder farm.

"Where do you think you're going?" Miriam demanded, grasping the side of the seat as he made the turn.

"Taking you home."

"This way?" She tried to sound stern, but it came out in a burst of amusement.

He had a silly smile on his face, like he was so proud of himself and of his clever bending of the rules. "I didn't say how long it would take me to get you home, did I?"

"You cheat," she protested. He'd let go of her hand when he was guiding the horse out of the barnyard and onto the blacktop, but now he grasped it again. She tried to pull away, but he held on tight. "Charley." Small sparks of pleasure ran up her arm. "Let me go."

"I don't want to," he answered. "You're too hard to catch."

She looked at him. "Maybe I don't want to be caught."

"Miriam, please. You've been running away from me for days." His tone turned serious. "Let me say what I have to say, before I lose my nerve."

The worn leather of the seat felt soft under her fingertips. "I can't remember you ever having trouble before talking to me."

"That's because you usually understand me so well. Sometimes you know what I'm thinking or how I'm feeling without me even having to say anything. So I *thought* when I told you about my new job that you'd understand."

"Understand what?"

"What I was trying to tell you." He groaned uncomfortably. "Miriam, I was trying to tell you that I want to court you."

For long seconds and then minutes, there was no sound but the creak of the buggy wheels, the rustle of the harness and the steady rhythm of the gelding's hooves on the roadway. Her mouth felt dry. Because Mam had warned her, she'd thought about what she was going to say when he asked her. She'd rehearsed how she was going to explain to Charley why she didn't want to walk out with him, but now that the time had come, she wasn't sure what to say. She didn't *know* what to say because she didn't know how she felt about the idea.

"Miriam," he said, finally breaking the awkward silence. "You're supposed to say something."

He was still holding her hand, his grasp warm and so...*nice*. "I...I'm thinking."

"So tell me what you're thinking."

"I'm thinking that I like you, Charley. We've always

been such good friends," she hedged. "But I never thought of us like that—courting."

"I understand that, but maybe you should. Friendship is a place to start. It wouldn't be much sense to court if we hated each other. Do you hate me?"

She shook her head. "You know better than that. It's just that courting, marriage, they're big steps." She felt emotion welling up in her throat. She felt so awful for saying this, for hurting Charley, because she knew she was, but she had to be truthful with him, didn't she? "The truth is," she blurted, "I don't know what I want...or *who* I want."

He threaded the lines through his fingers and slowed the horse to a walk. His voice remained calm, not squeaky like hers had become. "You've been walking out with John."

"No, I haven't," she protested. "I rode to Easton with him. We had lunch in a restaurant. That was all."

"And you had a good time?"

She took a deep breath. This was so hard, being completely honest. With herself and with Charley. "Yes," she admitted, "I did."

"Did he kiss you?"

She stiffened, glancing at him. "That's none of your business."

"Well, just in case." He knotted the lines around the dash rail, slid over and took her in his arms.

Before she could muster a protest, Charley leaned close and kissed her. His mouth was warm, his breath clean. Without realizing she was going to do it, she leaned forward and kissed him back. Their lips fit together perfectly, and sweet tingly sensations made her giddy.

Breathless, she pushed him away. "Do you make

a habit of kissing the girls you drive home from sing-ings?"

"I suppose I do." He chuckled in the darkness as he took the reins again. The horse had never broken stride.

"Charley Byler!"

"I'm kidding. You're the first, Miriam, the first girl I ever kissed. Just now." He grinned.

She folded her arms over her chest, trying to convince herself that she didn't like it...that she didn't want him to kiss her again. "That's not true," she accused. "What about Ada Peachy? I saw you kiss her behind the school-house at the seventh grade picnic."

"Doesn't count," he argued firmly. "She kissed me. Missed my mouth and kissed my nose. I ran away." He took hold of her hand again and gently squeezed it.

She pulled her hand away from his, but only after she savored the feel of it for a second. "Why did you kiss me? Because we have no chaperone? Because you think I'm wild enough to do anything?"

He chuckled. "Because I've wanted to kiss you for a long time. A very long time. And because I want to marry you."

"Take me home, Charley."

"Will you?"

"Marry you?" she asked, incredulously.

"Well, yes. But that's not my question, for now. My question, for tonight, is will you think about letting me court you?"

She knotted her fingers together, still able to feel the heat of his hand on hers and the taste of his mouth. Her heart was beating faster than the horse's hooves were striking the road.

She wanted to refuse. She'd been practically forced to

ride home with him, and he'd taken advantage of that by kissing her. Wasn't that reason enough to say no?

She brushed her lower lip with a fingertip. But maybe, just maybe, there was more to this man beside her than she'd imagined, and maybe she'd be a fool not to give him the chance to prove it. Making up her mind, she raised a finger to him. "No more kisses," she warned.

He nodded. "No more kisses until we're pledged."

"No one said anything about pledging *or* courting. I'm promising nothing tonight but an open mind. You can come around, sometimes, but you can't tell people that we're courting, because we're not. Now, turn the buggy around and take me home."

"*Ya,* Miriam, whatever you say." He chuckled, lifting the reins. "But you must admit, it was a *very* nice kiss."

The following day was Sunday, not the worship Sabbath but the day for relaxation and visiting with family and friends. After breakfast, Miriam took the buggy and picked up Johanna and the children, which was their usual routine on off Sundays. Johanna loved nothing more than spending time with her mother and sisters, and Wilmer seemed equally satisfied with the arrangement.

"Wilmer likes to spend the Lord's Day in peace and quiet, not listening to babies wail," Johanna explained on the way home. "He studies German, reads his Bible studies and writes to his family in Kentucky."

"Mmm," Miriam agreed. "They do get noisy." Jonah was standing between her knees, his small hands on the leathers, pretending to drive Blackie.

"Sometimes," Johanna agreed.

She was wearing a maroon dress, white apron and *kapp,* all clean and starched, but worn. Her shoes, Miriam noticed, were the same navy sneakers she wore every day, and they had seen better days, as well. Wilmer made a good living on his construction job, but he was frugal with his money when it came to his wife and children. It annoyed Miriam that Wilmer was a spiffy dresser for an Amish man, but the only new clothes her sister ever got were the ones Mam made for her. She'd have to mention Johanna's shoes to their mother.

"Get up!" Jonah shouted and shook the leathers. The gelding broke into a trot and the boy laughed.

"Easy," Miriam soothed. "You must be gentle. Never jerk on the reins. It hurts the animal's mouth." She took a firm hand on the lines as a pickup passed the carriage.

"Ya," Jonah agreed. "Okay."

Katie, seated on her mother's lap, laughed, kicked her feet and waved her arms. She was a happy, chubby-cheeked baby with bright eyes and an adorable laugh.

"How did it go last night? With Charley?" Johanna bounced Katie on her knee. "I've been waiting to hear."

"It went all right." She glanced at her sister. "But that was rotten of you, to tell him that I'd ride home with him from the singing without my say-so."

Johanna shrugged. "Just doing my job as your big sister. You shouldn't be too quick to pick a husband."

"Who says I am?"

Katie yanked her *kapp* off and threw it in the air. Johanna caught it and plopped it back on the baby's head. *"Ne.* You must wear your head covering, sweetie."

Miriam looked at Johanna. "What makes you think I've picked a husband?"

"Mary. Charley's sister. She said John and you were walking out. That he was courting you." Johanna's expression turned serious. "You need to make certain it's what you want. You shouldn't decide against Charley without putting some serious thought into it."

Becoming frustrated, Miriam gripped the reins tighter. "Who was it who told me to go with John to Easton? You! Now you're trying to force Charley on me?" She stared at the road straight ahead. "Which one do you want me to go with? John or Charley?"

"Both. Neither." Johanna placed a firm hand on Jonah's shoulder. "Do not jump up and down. If you can't behave, you'll have to sit in the back of the buggy."

"I'm good," Jonah protested, and immediately stopped hopping.

"*Ya,* you are a good boy. *Most* of the time. But you have to be careful in the buggy. Do you want to fall and have the wheels run over your noodle?"

Jonah giggled.

"I've got him." Miriam wrapped an arm around the child's waist.

Johanna returned her attention to her sister. "So what do you think about Charley?"

"I don't know what I think."

Johanna shifted Katie to her shoulder. "And John?"

"I don't know that, either."

"Good," Johanna pronounced. "So, it's best that you see both of them. Go places, do things, have fun, with both of them. Be certain in your heart before you choose."

"But how will I know? I like them both," Miriam admitted. "John's exciting, and Charley's…" She leaned close to her sister's ear. "He kissed me on the way home last night."

Johanna's eyes narrowed and she glanced at her son. "How was it?" she whispered.

"Nice."

"All right, then. Now, the thing to do is to kiss John and see how they match up."

"Johanna!" Miriam glanced at her sister, then at the road again. "What would Mam say? What kind of advice is that for a big sister to give her younger one? Would you have people say I'm fast?"

"Better fast than foolish."

Chapter Twelve

The following day, Charley stopped by his brother Roland's house after supper. He'd intended on visiting Miriam, but as he was walking down the road, halfway to her house, John had passed him in his truck. John backed up and asked if Charley wanted a ride, explaining that he was going by the Yoders' to check on Molly.

Not wanting to share Miriam with John, Charley had changed his original plans. "Thanks just the same," he'd said. "But I'm on my way to Roland's." John had offered to give him a lift to Roland's driveway, but he'd refused that, too, saying that he needed to stretch his legs.

It wasn't exactly the whole truth, but close enough. And now that he was here in his brother's kitchen, bouncing his nephew, Jared, on his knee, Charley was glad he'd come. Pauline, Roland's wife, was expecting twins and wasn't well. She was lying down and Roland was cleaning up the supper dishes.

"Ride a horse, ride a horse," Charley said to little Jared, and then swung him high in the air. "And don't let him throw you!"

Jared squealed with laughter. "More! More!" he demanded in the German dialect the English called

Pennsylvania Dutch. Jared was too young to speak or understand English. Most Amish children learned it in the first grade when they went to school, although Charley and Roland's mother had taught them both English and German from babyhood on.

"Enough, enough," Roland protested. "It's his bedtime."

Charley noticed that the boy was already bathed and in a clean nightshirt and diaper. "You have this routine down good," he said, handing the giggling child over to his father.

Roland lifted Jared onto his shoulders. "A family's needs must be met, brother. Give me a few minutes to tuck him in. Pour yourself some coffee. I'll be down as quick as I can."

While Roland went upstairs, Charley picked up a dish towel, dried the knives and forks on the counter and put them away. He found a broom and swept the kitchen before helping himself to the coffee on the back of the stove. When Roland returned, Charley saw that his brother's face looked troubled.

"We were all praying that the new endocrinologist would help Pauline," Charley said. "I hear Bishop Atlee goes to him."

Roland nodded. "I feel bad, brother. Her condition. It would have been better for her if she hadn't gotten pregnant again, but..." He shrugged. "The doctor seems good, but carrying two babies is hard on her, what with her diabetes. The midwife tells us that they may come too soon."

"It's a terrible disease."

Charley knew that Pauline had needed to take insulin daily since she was a teenager, but she'd seemed so much better in the first year of her marriage. Now, she'd gotten worse—a lot worse—and Roland's medical bills were mounting. The Amish carried no health insurance as the English did. Instead, the community pitched in when there was a need.

"*Ya.* My wife is a good wife and mother. She wanted more babies so badly." Roland looked around the kitchen. "You swept? No need for that. I was going to do it."

"It's not easy for you, either, Roland. When Mam hears—"

"*Ne.* Don't worry her. Pauline's sisters have been a help with Jared. We're making out. It's good you stopped by. We don't get enough time to talk. Remember when we were kids? It seemed like we were never apart."

Charley laughed. "I remember. You were always getting me out of one scrape or another. And you were always giving me advice to keep me out of trouble."

"Which you *never* listened to. Always the jokes and teasing for Charley." Roland lit an oil lamp. It cast a yellow circle of light across the table and began to smoke until he turned down the wick. "It can't go on, you know." Roland peered over the top of his glasses and fiddled with the wick again. "Time you settle down, get baptized and start courting that pretty Yoder girl."

"Which one?" They both laughed. Roland knew which Yoder girl Charley fancied. But then, *everyone* knew.

"Seriously, little brother. You've got that steady job you were wanting. If you're not careful, someone else will snatch her away. Maybe even that John Hartman."

Charley slid his cup away and met his brother's steady gaze. Behind Roland's thick glasses were big blue eyes, full of wisdom and compassion. "I asked her if I could court her," Charley admitted. "I even kissed her. Just once. When I drove her home from the singing last night."

Roland tugged at his short beard. "Not something I'd mention to Preacher Reuben if I were you. She let you?"

Charley shrugged. "I think she liked it as much as I did, even though she acted mad afterward." He was quiet for a second. "But that's not the thing. You know, I've always expected that we'd marry, someday. Everybody knows it. Didn't I buy Miriam's pie last spring at the school fundraising picnic so I could eat with her? Right in front of everyone?"

"That you did. So, what's your problem?"

Charley brought his palms together as if in prayer, before lightly tapping his chin with his index fingers. "Now that I've finally gotten around to asking her if I can walk out with her, she doesn't seem all that interested. I think that Mennonite has stolen my thunder."

"More like, your girl." Roland got up, went to the refrigerator and brought back a blueberry pie and two forks. "Help me eat this," he said. "Mam keeps sending pies over. Pauline can't eat them and they're making me fat."

Charley looked at the pie. "So you want to make *me* fat?"

"Blueberries. They give you brain power."

"Which I'm lacking, compared to the *veterinarian*," Charley took one of the forks and cut off a mouthful of pie.

"*Ne.* That's not true. You were always the smart one in the family. Who won the eighth grade spelling bee?"

Charley grimaced. "Miriam."

"Okay, bad example. But you always got a hundred percent on your fractions and long division. And that doesn't really matter, not when it comes to being a good husband. You just need to figure out how to show Miriam that *you'll* make a better husband than John will."

"Not easy." Charley forked pie into his mouth and chewed. "Competition's stiff. He's got that truck and he makes more money than I do. They're both interested in healing animals. I don't even have a house to take her to, if she *would* marry me."

Roland tossed him a paper napkin. "Blueberry. There on your chin."

Charley laughed, wiping his chin. "Flaky. Mam makes good pies."

"You ever think maybe you don't need a house? Who does all the cooking at the Yoder place?"

"Mostly Anna, I guess. Sometimes Hannah. The other girls pitch in."

"And who does most of the outside chores? Putting in the crops? Milking the cows?"

"Miriam. She's always liked farming better than housework. And she's good at it. Did you see her corn crop last year?"

"My point. And how well do you get along with her mother?"

"Hannah? Fine. Who doesn't like—" Charley broke off and stared at Roland. "You mean…live there? At the Yoder place?"

"Why not? If it suits Miriam, why not? So long as Hannah is all right with it. They could certainly use another man for the heavy work, and it's a big house."

"It is. Miriam said they don't even use the rooms over the kitchen. And there's the *Grossdaadi haus*. We might—"

"*Ne.*" Roland shook his head. "Mam said that Alma said that her mother and aunt might be coming to live with Hannah, once her mother-in-law can travel. I got the idea that there were some problems the Yoder girls in Ohio were dealing with, but Mam didn't say what."

"Hannah's going to take her in? A daughter-in-law? Why don't Alma or Martha take her? *They're* her daughters."

"Alma told Mam that Lovina can't stand her, and she never did get along with Martha."

"I've seen enough of Lovina to know she can be a handful, plus there's her sister, Jezebel. A lot for Hannah and the girls."

Roland smiled. "All the more reason it would make sense for you to help out by staying on the farm. What with you having a steady job now, it makes more sense than you taking Miriam home to Mam and Dat's. Can you see our father letting Miriam plow his fields?"

"Hardly." Charley grinned at the thought. "It does seem sensible. But how does that help my immediate problem of getting Miriam to agree to let me court her? How can I compete with John? She likes him a lot, and they've got taking care of animals in common. Plus, he's such a good guy. He helped out with the house-raising and he even brought Eli and Ruth that bathroom stuff."

"John is worldly, and a good man, that's true enough. But it would be a big step for Miriam to leave the Amish faith. Don't be so quick to give up, brother. Put your trust in God to do the right thing for all of you. If He means for Miriam to be your wife, no one can come between you."

"But *John* is coming between us, Roland. Chances are, he's standing there in the Yoder barn with her, *right this minute.*"

"So why are you here?" Roland stood up. "Get on over there, boy. Let her see that you care about her. And don't try to be someone you're not. She can depend on you, Charley. You're steady. Make certain she remembers that." He went back to the refrigerator, took out another blueberry pie and handed it to him. "Here, take this. It will give you an excuse for coming over so late."

Charley clutched the pie. "You think I should?"

Roland opened the kitchen door. "Get going, before she starts kissing John."

And for once, Charley did as Roland advised.

Late Tuesday afternoon, Miriam was cleaning Molly's stall when her mother came into the barn, a kerchief tied over her head and picked up a pitchfork.

"Mam, I can do this. There's no need for you to—"

"You think I don't know how to muck a stall?" Her mother smiled. "Sometimes hard work is what we need." She scooped up a heap of dirty straw and dumped it into the wheelbarrow. "So how is the mare? Will the infection heal?"

Miriam nodded. "It looks like it will. She's much better. John expects her to make a full recovery in a few weeks."

"He comes a lot, John."

"He cares about Molly."

Her mother leaned on her pitchfork. "He comes to see more than the mare, I think."

Miriam didn't answer. They continued working, side by side.

"Aunt Martha told me that the neighbors wonder why the vet comes here so much for a sore hoof. You know how people like to talk, to gossip."

Miriam pushed the gate open and pulled the wheelbarrow out into the passageway. "That should do it. I'll go up into the loft for fresh straw."

Her mother stepped in front of her, blocking her way. "We have to talk about this, child."

"I'm not a child." Miriam rested one hand on her hip. She was taller than her mother, but only by an inch. "I'm twenty-one. I know what I'm doing."

"So, all grown up, you are? No longer need a mother's advice?"

"It's because John's Mennonite, isn't it?" She looked into her mother's face. "You were once Mennonite. Were you ungodly? Is he a bad man because he wasn't born Amish?"

"No one said anything about ungodly. Come." Hannah took her hand and led her to a hay bale. "Sit," she said.

Miriam sat. "Mam, you don't understand. John is—"

"Listen to me," her mother interrupted. "Do you love him with all your heart? Are you ready to leave your family, your church, everything you know for *his* world?"

"I don't know. I *like* him a lot. I feel all giddy when I see him. He makes me laugh, and…"

"He's new and exciting."

Miriam nodded. "So many things he takes for granted, things I would like to do and see. But how can I be sure?"

Hannah grasped her hand and squeezed it. "When I met your father, Jonas, it was the same way for me. This world…" She glanced around the barn. "This quiet, peaceful world, it was different than what I'd grown up with."

"But your life revolved around God, too." Miriam stared at the dirt floor. "How did you know that Dat was the one man for you?"

"Like you, there was another boy that favored me.

His family and mine were close. They'd served on a mission with us to Canada. My mother wanted me to marry him."

"You went to Canada? You never told us that." Miriam's eyes widened. "Why didn't I know that? Where in Canada? How old were you?"

"It was long ago. Our work was with the Indian people in the north. I don't remember a lot, just the games I played with the tribal children and the cold winters. Two years, we were there. We came back when I was eight." She grew thoughtful. "It isn't just John that the community is talking about. Charley was here last night, too, wasn't he?"

Miriam nodded. "He came just after John left. He brought us one of his mother's blueberry pies."

"If you are thinking seriously of John, is it fair to encourage Charley?"

"The problem is that I can't say I don't want to encourage Charley, too."

"It isn't the custom to walk out with two boys at the same time. Some consider that fast, for a girl. Not Plain."

Miriam scuffed her shoe in the straw. "I haven't joined the church. I don't have to follow the rules yet."

"The Amish way is not an easy one. It's not for everybody. It may not be your way. It's the reason I haven't pressed for you to be baptized yet. I wanted you to embrace our faith with your whole heart, to realize that the rules are not walls but wings that will someday lift you to heaven."

She looked at her mother. "Have you ever been sorry that you left the Mennonites to become Amish?" It was something that she'd always wanted to ask, but had been afraid to.

Hannah shook her head. "Never. Not even when I lost my dear partner, not even when some of my family closed their doors to me and my children. It was the right thing for me. I had dreamed of being a missionary to faraway lands, and instead I found joy here, in this tranquil place."

"If I choose John, will you close your door to me, Mam?"

"Never." She grabbed Miriam's hand, squeezed it and let it go. "And neither will your sisters. But do not join the church and then leave. So long as you are not baptized in our faith, the leaders cannot shun you. You will always be welcome at home."

"What do you think of Charley?"

"As a man or as your husband?" Mam asked. She went on before Miriam could answer. "He has a good heart. And he's a hard worker. You will never go hungry if you marry Charley. He's also generous, with his feelings and material things. You'll never wear old shoes while he wears new."

Mam's words were the closest Miriam had ever heard her speak against Johanna's husband. But Miriam was sure she was not mistaken. Mam was referring to Wilmer.

"But the problem is, I like them both," Miriam explained. "How do I know which one is best for me?"

"It would mean two very different ways of life."

Miriam sighed. "I realize that, Mam. But I can't decide which one I'd be happier with." She swallowed, trying to dissolve the constriction in her throat. "How do I know what God wants me to do?"

"It's not easy. He has given us free will, and with that comes the possibility of choosing wrong and having to live with the consequences."

"You want me to pick Charley, don't you?"

Mam chuckled. "I want you to pick the man who will make you the happiest. I want you to marry the man who will help you become the woman God intends you to be."

"But I don't know who that is. John hasn't even asked to court me. I think he wants to—I know he does. But he hasn't said it in so many words."

"And Charley did?"

"Yes, but he asked you first. He's asked everyone. I'd be surprised if he hasn't asked Uncle Reuben's permission." She pushed back hair that had escaped from her kerchief. "How can I know what's right when everyone is pushing me into Charley's arms?"

Her mother got to her feet. "I would tell you to pray, but I know you have prayed and will continue to do so. Know that I pray for you, and your sisters do, too. But no one can make this decision but you."

Miriam nodded thoughtfully. "So maybe I have to make my own rules. Decide my own way."

"Take your time. And whatever decision you make, I will always love you as much as I love you at this moment."

"I guess I need to find out John's intentions, don't I?" She was speaking as much to herself, as to her mother.

Mam smiled. "That would seem to be a good place to start." She leaned close and kissed Miriam's cheek. "I have faith in you, daughter. You have a good head on your shoulders. You'll figure this out."

"I hope so," Miriam said.

Her mind was already racing. What *was* wrong with having two boys court her at once? She didn't give a rotten apple for what Aunt Martha and the other gossips thought. What she needed to do was find out exactly how

John felt about her. And if he wasn't truly interested in a serious relationship that might lead to marriage, then her question would be answered—at least as far as John was concerned.

As for Charley, he remained an equally big question, but for different reasons. Was he really just a friend, as she had insisted to everyone, including herself? Or was he more? *That* she'd have to think about.

Chapter Thirteen

Miriam waited until her mother and sisters had retired to bed before retreating to Johanna's old bedroom over the kitchen. The only way to reach this portion of the house was through the kitchen and up the back staircase. Although the rooms were furnished, this area was rarely used since Johanna had married and Leah and Rebecca remained with *Grossmama*. It was the only place in the house that was private enough for the phone call Miriam wanted to make to John.

Deciding to ask him his intentions was frightening. Actually doing it was more so. Her fingers trembled as she waited for him to answer.

"Miriam?"

"*Ya*, John. It is me." He'd been there earlier in the evening tending to Molly. Obviously, he hadn't expected her to call. "Am I bothering you?"

"No, of course not. Wait. I'll walk outside," he said. Miriam heard footsteps and the creak of a door, then the sound of his boots on the wooden porch. "All right." John chuckled. "I didn't want my grandfather listening in. And he would."

She took a deep breath. Why was this so awkward?

Earlier, in the barn, they'd laughed and talked easily. She'd leaned on the stall door as John had brushed Molly's hide until she shone. "I have a question to ask you," she said.

"Okay." He sounded curious, but amused, too.

"Do you like me? But not just *like*…" She caught her lower lip between her teeth. "John, is it more than *like?*" She took a deep breath and just said it. "Do you want to court me?"

There was a moment of silence long enough to make her wish she could shrink down to the size of a mouse and crawl away.

Then he chuckled. "Isn't this conversation a little backward? I thought *I* was the one who was supposed to ask you about how you felt about *me*."

"This is not easy." Her knees felt weak, her palms sweaty. She sank down in the center of the braided rug. "I have to know, John. It's important. And…and if I was wrong to think that you—"

"You aren't wrong. I think…" It sounded as if he took a deep breath. "Miriam, I think I may be in love with you."

How sweet those words sounded. But she had to be sure what he meant. "Love is one thing," she said hesitantly. "Courting and marriage are another. I have to know if you're serious."

"I'm serious." He spoke firmer now. "I would like to court you, Miriam Yoder—walk out with you. Whatever you call it. I like you better than any girl I've ever met. Seeing you is the highlight of my day. That said, I have a question for you. Have you thought about how difficult this would be? Our families…"

"It's *all* I think about. But I want to know you better— to be alone with you, see more of your world. I don't know if it's love I feel. I think it is, John, but I want to be sure."

"So do I."

She felt warm all over now. Still a little nervous, but a good nervous. "You're not angry, that I asked you this?"

"Nothing you do or say could make me angry, Miriam."

"Don't be so fast to say that." She hesitated. "Because you should know that Charley has already asked to court me."

More silence. And when John finally spoke, his voice had lost the easy, teasing tone. She could almost see his shoulders tightening, his lips thinning. "And what did you tell him? Did you say yes?"

She lay back on the rug. "It would be easy if I liked Charley best. My family would like that. My church. They expect me to marry Charley or someone like him. Me, I don't know what I want. I like Charley, but I don't know that he makes me feel the way you do," she dared.

"So?"

She exhaled. "So I need to find out."

"You want to date both of us?" John sounded out of sorts now, almost cross.

"I think it would be best," she said. "Maybe I am in love with you…or maybe it is your world I love. And maybe, with Charley…maybe with Charley, I haven't given him a real chance, because I already know his world. Our world."

"What we're talking about is some sort of competition, here. I thought the Amish didn't go for competition—that it wasn't Plain."

A wave of sadness brought tears to sting the back

of her eyelids. "You're angry with me." She could see him in her mind's eye, his broad forehead, the curve of his bottom lip. Her heart plunged. What if she'd ruined everything by being too forward?

"Just surprised. This is a lot to take in."

"Too much, maybe. It could be that this would never work for either of us. For me to walk in your world...for you to fit in mine."

"Yes," he agreed. "I see that." Emotion made his voice deepen. "But I'll do whatever I have to. I'll prove to you that I'd be the best husband for you. I'm not going to give you up without a fight."

"We do not fight. And I don't believe it is the Mennonite way, either. And this isn't a *competition*. It's important that we both go into this with our eyes open. For me, marriage is forever, John. If I choose you, I will never walk away from you. I will honor and cherish you all the days of my life."

"Me, too. What other people think doesn't matter. It's you and me, what we want. It's our life."

"*Ne,* John. Our life includes our families, our church. Most importantly, I must be certain that I choose the path that God intends for me."

"I respect that. But do you think you could become Mennonite? I can't see you remaining Amish if we're together. It would be too difficult for our children."

"I've thought of that," she assured him. "It's a real consideration."

"I don't attend services as regularly as I should. It's only fair that you know that being part of the church isn't as important to me as it is to you."

"I don't know if I could leave the Amish faith, but if I change to a more liberal church, it wouldn't mean forgetting God's part in my life."

"I wouldn't ask you to."

Her stomach was still queasy, but she was beginning to feel hopeful again. "I told my mother that I care for you. She advised me to be certain. You know she was raised Mennonite and converted for my father."

"Uncle Albert told me that."

"So, she knows what it's like to make such a difficult decision. If we…if we *date,* we will come to know each other better, to see if what you feel…if what *I* feel is the love that makes a marriage."

"Wow. Heavy stuff."

She laughed softly. "But this will be Amish dating. Not English."

"Mennonite?"

"Maybe. We will see. But I cannot shame my family. We must do nothing that will disgrace them—or us. We have to be chaperoned."

"Chaperoned?" He laughed. "We weren't chaperoned when we went to Easton."

"That was different. It wasn't a *date.* And it was during the day."

"I don't really understand the difference. We were still alone."

She nibbled on her lower lip. "It's complicated, John. A lot of it has to do with appearances."

"What have I got myself into?"

She dared a little smile. "That's what I intend to find out."

"So, next weekend. Will you go out with me?" he asked. "On a date?"

"Sunday is church. Saturday, I will be free."

"Saturday it is then. Would you like to go to the beach? The amusement rides are still open on the weekends. Ferris wheel? Carousel? Are you game?"

"*Ya,* John. I will go with you. It sounds like fun. I've never been on a Ferris wheel. Can we eat hot dogs and salt water taffy and candy cotton?"

"All the candy cotton you want." He chuckled. "But one thing I insist on."

"And that is?"

"Charley Byler cannot go with us to the beach."

She giggled. "I agree. No Charley."

It was Thursday morning before Charley made it back to the Yoder farm to finish the back steps on Eli and Ruth's new house. Miriam waited until Mam and Irwin had gone to school and Susanna, Ruth and Anna were busy with the washing before walking across the field toward the little house. She carried a cup of coffee as an excuse, in case she lost her nerve. "Morning, Charley," she said, coming around the corner of the house. "I brought you coffee."

He looked up at her and grinned. "And I was just sitting here thinking how much I'd like to have a second cup. I only had time for one this morning before I left."

Miriam smiled back. She'd been annoyed with Charley for so long that she'd forgotten how sweet his smile was. She felt a rush of affection and realized that no matter how much she'd denied it, she did care for Charley. But how could she like Charley if she was in love with John? Suddenly, her plan, which had seemed so sensible, seemed to leave her more confused than ever. Did she like either of them enough to marry, or was she so fickle that she'd become infatuated with any good-looking boy who glanced her way? Maybe Aunt Martha was right, and she was *fast*.

Charley stood and wiped his broad hands on his canvas apron. He'd been laying bricks and bits of cement clung to his trousers and shirt. "Appreciate this," he said. "The coffee…and a chance to talk to you alone."

She looked at the steps. How could she make him understand what she was about to say? "Good job." She pointed to his masonry. "Solid. I can see Ruth running up and down them."

"It's a good house." He took a sip of the coffee and looked at her.

She felt herself blush. "I didn't come just to bring you coffee," she said.

He grinned again, removed his straw hat and wiped his forehead with the back of his hand. "It's going to be hot today."

"Don't you want to know why I came?"

Charley chuckled. "I figured you'd tell me in your own good time."

She sat down on the grass and picked a cloverleaf. "Were you serious when you asked if you could court me?"

His blue eyes narrowed. "What do you think?"

She met his gaze. "I've decided you can, if you want to."

"What?"

"You can court me—walk out with me."

"Hmm." He regarded her thoughtfully. "What convinced you? My fancy way with brick steps or the kiss in the buggy?"

"Charley Byler! How can you bring up such a thing?"

"How can you forget it?"

She felt her cheeks grow as warm as the grass she sat in. "It isn't proper to talk about such things." She put her hand on her hip. "So now I suppose you think I'm wild? So you won't want to court me anymore?" She was teasing him, of course. Giving him a taste of his own medicine.

He reached forward to catch her hand, but she was too quick for him. She twisted away, but before she could scoot back, he caught hold of one bare foot. "*Ya,* Miriam. I do. I want you more than anything; I want you to be my wife."

"Let go of me, Charley Byler! My foot's dirty." She struggled to break free.

"*Ne, ne,* just stay and talk to me."

"Let me go first." He did as she asked and she scrambled to her feet and backed away. "Are you crazy?"

"I'd never do anything to hurt you. You know that. You know how I feel about you."

"Then keep your hands off me." Now she planted both hands on her hips. "What's come over you?"

"You have, Miriam. You make me crazy…thinking about you all the time…wondering if I have a chance with you."

"If I agree to walk out with you, there's something you should know."

"I get another kiss?"

It was all she could do to not laugh. Where did he get the nerve? "You *do not,*" she said, with more feeling than she felt. "That was a mistake."

He sighed dramatically. "I can hold your hand?"

She shook her head. "And not my foot, either." She took a step toward him, looked up, then down at the ground. "There is something else, though. About John."

His brow furrowed. "What about John?"

"I might be in love with him."

"You might love John, yet you want me to court you?" He looked at her as if she were the one acting crazy.

She nodded. "It's the only way. I want to walk out with you both. And then I can choose. Once I know which one is right for me."

Hurt flashed in his eyes and he turned back to his work. Without another word, he picked up the trowel, scooped up cement and tapped it onto the top of a brick.

"You don't have to, if you don't want to," she said, drawing closer.

"You want to court both of us?"

"Mam knows."

"It will cause talk."

"Some people always gossip."

"They will say you are wild and I am a fool." He slammed the brick into place.

"No one who knows you will say you're a fool, Charley. And we will be properly chaperoned."

"Just you and me, or you and the Mennonite?"

"Both. I don't want to cause a scandal. I just want to be certain."

"And if I refuse to be a part of this nonsense?"

"I will be sorry, but I'll still walk out with John."

"And he's agreed to this?"

"John? *Ya.* He has."

"Then he is a fool."

"Charley! What a thing to say."

"What a thing to do." He looked back at her. "You are not like every other Amish girl."

"Maybe not," she said. Then she dared a little smile. "But that's what you like about me."

Chapter Fourteen

Susanna squealed with joy as the Ferris wheel turned, lifting them in the air before pausing, suspending them high over the amusement park. It was twilight and everywhere below, lights were blinking on. Miriam could still make out the ocean to the east and the narrow white ribbon of sand along the water's edge.

The basket swayed and Susanna clutched Miriam's hand. "Falling!"

"No," John assured her. "We won't fall. Look, you can see the merry-go-round. Hear the music?"

"Music," Susanna agreed. "I like the *merry-go-around*. I want to go down."

Miriam slipped an arm around her sister's shoulders. "We won't fall," she assured her. "It's all right, Susanna."

"I want to go down," Susanna said. "My tummy hurts."

Miriam looked at John. "I warned you not to buy her more cotton candy."

John smiled. "She'll be fine, won't you, Susanna? You're just like a bird, flying in the air, round and round."

John's hand covered Miriam's and Susanna's, and Miriam felt a little thrill at his touch. She'd deliberately put her sister between them. It was too easy to be intimate on these rides and she didn't want to be tempted. In spite of Susanna's fears, they were both having a wonderful time.

The day had been one marvel after another. Susanna had laughed at herself in the silly curved mirrors. They'd thrown balls at silly red and yellow wooden clowns, and she'd beaten John. She'd knocked every one down and won the prize—a stuffed bear that she gave to a little Hispanic girl in a red dress who'd been cheering her on. John had treated them to pizza, the sweet that she'd learned was called cotton candy—not candy cotton— and a frozen chocolate banana on a stick. They'd ridden the merry-go-round and played miniature golf on the roof of a building, with the ocean as a backdrop. She'd beaten John at the golf game as well, and he'd teased her about it. Best of all, they'd taken off their shoes and walked down to wade in the waves that washed against the beach.

The Ferris wheel began to rotate again. Susanna screamed as the rocking basket descended toward the ground and then rose again, even faster. Salt air blew against Miriam's face, threatening to tear away her *kapp* and send it flying through the night sky. With her free hand, she grabbed the knot under her chin and held tight. The earth rose to meet them at a frightening speed. When the Ferris wheel finally came to a stop, she was dizzy and her first steps were unsteady.

John caught her arm. "Easy. We can't have you taking a tumble," he said.

Now that they were back on firm ground, Susanna's

fears appeared to have dissolved. "Let's go again!" she urged, clapping her hands and doing a little dance from side to side. "Let's go again."

"That's enough for one night." Miriam straightened her sister's *kapp* and tied it firmly to keep it from blowing away in the stiff breeze.

A sunburned couple in shorts and sweatshirts gawked and pointed at Susanna, but whether they were staring at her Amish clothing or because she had Down syndrome, Miriam didn't know. When the woman fished a camera out of her purse and aimed it in Susanna's direction, John stepped in front of Susanna, blocking the shot. The man said something rude, and Miriam could see John quickly losing his temper.

Miriam took hold of Susanna's hand and tucked her free arm through the inside of his elbow. "Let's go. We have to get up early in the morning for church."

"I'm sorry about those people," John said, hustling them away from the Englishers.

"It's not your fault," Miriam said. "It happens all the time." She would have let go of John's arm, but he held her firmly. A small flush of excitement made her giddy, and she hoped he wouldn't think she was too forward.

Susanna's short legs pumped as she hurried to keep up. "We're gonna ride in the blue truck!"

"Yes," John agreed. "In the blue truck."

"Can I blow the horn?" Susanna begged. "Can I?"

"Ne," Miriam said. "The horn is for emergencies. We could frighten another driver."

"Or a horse," Susanna said.

"Or a horse," John agreed.

Miriam glanced at him. "It was a lovely day. Thank

you for taking us." They walked out of the noisy building with its flashing lights and loud music, back to the truck parked on the street.

"Can we come again tomorrow?" Susanna asked. "I like the merry-go-around. I want to ride the white horse with the bell."

Soon they were driving down Rehoboth Avenue in light traffic. Susanna's nose was pressed against the truck window, staring at the tourists that crowded the sidewalks and flowed onto the street. "That girl is in her underpants!" Susanna declared. "Where's her dress?"

"Shh, don't look. She's English," Miriam explained, clapping a hand over her sister's eyes. "That's her swimming suit."

Susanna wiggled aside so that she could see. "But I can see her— She's bad."

"Not bad," John corrected. "Just not Plain. They're different."

"She's silly," Susanna said. "Fast."

"Susanna," Miriam admonished. "We don't talk about people."

"But—"

"Shh."

John chuckled. "She's right. The girl is silly. She'd be prettier with more clothes on."

"Do you really think so?" Miriam asked.

"I do. I think you're beautiful, just as you are."

They rode in silence for a little while, and soon Susanna was asleep, her head on Miriam's shoulder.

"Did you have fun?" John asked, quietly.

Miriam nodded. "I've been to the ocean before, but never Fun Land. I had a wonderful time."

"Have you ever been swimming?"

"*Ya*. Sometimes we go to a little beach on the bay. Not

with swimming suits, but in our clothes. My sisters and I play in the water."

"My mother has a swimming pool in her yard. I could take you there. I know she has extra suits for my sisters."

Miriam chuckled. "Not for me. The Old Order Amish are more…more conservative than the more liberal Mennonite churches, I think. I don't judge girls who wish to wear revealing clothing, but we are taught to dress modestly."

"No swimming."

"No swimming in bathing costumes," she corrected him.

"Got it." He smiled at her in the darkness. "There's a charity spaghetti dinner at Uncle Albert's church next Friday night. Would you like to come?"

"The Mennonite church?"

"Yes. But there won't be a regular church service. I think a missionary's going to give a PowerPoint presentation and a talk afterward."

"What's that? A PowerPoint presentation?"

He glanced at her, but didn't look as if he thought she was dumb for asking. "It's sort of like a slide show, only it's done on a personal computer and then shown on a movie screen. But we wouldn't have to stay for that, if you didn't want to," he said quickly. "Would you be allowed to come, do you think?"

"If I bring one of my sisters. There aren't rules against going to other church benefits, John. The Old Order Amish Church isn't as strict as you seem to think."

"I'd like you to meet some of the members. If you…if we decide to go to the Mennonite church, they'll be part of our community."

"I've been thinking a lot about that." Miriam spoke

softly, not wanting to wake Susanna. "I can't even imagine becoming part of a new church. It's such a big decision."

"You don't need to make it yet." He smiled at her. "Unless you don't like spaghetti."

"Love it," she confided. "And it's the one thing Mam never learned to cook. Hers is all tomatoey. But don't you dare tell her that I said so."

"Wouldn't think of it," he said, reaching down and taking her hand in his. "I'm so glad you came today. I had fun, too, a lot of fun."

Her breath caught in her throat. She and John were holding hands, and it made her feel warm and safe. "Even with Susanna along?"

He laughed. "Especially with Susanna."

"And we went up high! High!" Susanna exclaimed. It was Sunday morning and Mam, Irwin and Miriam's sisters were just leaving the house for church. Susanna was telling her mother for the fourth time about her ride on the Ferris wheel and the blue cotton candy John had bought her the night before.

Services were at Charley's parents' house today, and Miriam had hitched Blackie to the family buggy. Since Mam was bringing food to share at the noon meal, they had loaded the bowls and covered trays into the back of the carriage, along with the jars of lemonade and iced tea.

Miriam guided Blackie close to the back steps. "Everyone ready?" She yawned, covering her mouth with the back of her hand. It had been late when she'd gotten home from her date with John, and she'd lain awake for a long time thinking of all she'd seen and done…and thinking of John and what it would be like to be part of his world.

"Charley!" Susanna pointed. "Morning!"

"Morning, sunshine!"

Miriam turned to see him strolling around the corner of the barn, hands in his pockets. She glanced at Ruth, who shrugged and climbed up into the buggy. Miriam got down and walked across the yard. "Isn't church at your house?" she asked.

"*Ya*. I thought I could walk you there." He lifted one eyebrow. "Unless you're too tired after your Saturday night date."

"I'll be happy to walk with you. It will give me a chance to stretch my legs before services. Let me tell Mam."

"Maybe you need one of your sisters to walk with us, so that it doesn't worry your uncle Reuben?" Charley suggested.

"We'll be fine," she assured him.

If they cut across the fields, it was less than two miles to Charley's father's place, and the day was perfect—sunny, but not too hot, with just a hint of autumn in the air. The way led through the back pasture, over a stile that Dat had built, through Samuel's woods and past the school. Neither of them spoke. But surprisingly, she wanted to talk to Charley. She wanted to point out the warbler flitting through the bushes and the last of the summer's clover, bursting with white blossoms. And she wanted to tell Charley about the rude woman who'd wanted to take Susanna's picture at the amusement park.

Once they reached the road that ran in front of the school, they walked along it for a few hundred yards before taking a farm lane that crossed an English farmer's property. Miriam couldn't stand the silence between them any longer, she said, "Not so long ago and you were taking this lane every day to the schoolhouse."

"*Ya.* I was."

She waited. When he added nothing more, she had to force down her irritation. This walk had started out pleasantly, but she could tell now that Charley had a bee in his hat over something. She could see it in his face—in the way he held his mouth. "We waded in the waves yesterday. At the ocean. The water was warm."

"September. Should be."

She looked at him. "And you would know so much about the Atlantic Ocean?"

"As much as you."

"Don't be mean, Charley."

"Am I being mean? I came to walk you to church, didn't I?" He stooped and picked a dandelion blossom and then another. When he had three, he braided the stems together, and then handed them to her. "See, like an Englishman, I give you flowers."

She laughed. "Some bouquet."

That broke the ice. Soon they were teasing and chatting as they had before Charley had ruined everything by asking if he could court her. She liked Charley like this: familiar, sweet, funny.

"Fish are biting good in Dat's pond," he said. "Maybe tomorrow, after supper, we could try and catch a few bass."

"Mam likes fish. It would be good if I could catch enough for breakfast."

"Bring Irwin. We'll make him clean the fish."

"He'll love that."

"Can you clean fish?" He stopped, pushed the brim of his hat up with a forefinger and looked at her.

"Sure. Dat taught me when I was little."

"And I can clean fish. So it's only fair we give Irwin the chance to learn how to do it, isn't it? And it will give him something to complain about, so he'll be happy."

Miriam chuckled. "He does whine a lot. I think he does it to get attention."

"Exactly." Charley tugged her bonnet string. "So we're building his character. Something even your uncle Reuben would approve of."

She tried to look serious. "This is Sunday. We're on our way to church. It's not a time to poke fun at a preacher."

Charley shook his head. "I wouldn't think of it. Preacher Reuben is a wise man. He'd be happy that we're taking an interest in Irwin—taking him fishing, having him along as a chaperone *and* showing him the value of work."

She brushed a piece of straw off her Sunday apron. "It sounds right when you say it like that, but I don't trust you. You're always up to something."

"Ne." Charley started walking again, matching his longer strides to her shorter ones. "I'll come for you both in Dat's buggy if you want."

"No need. We can roller-skate as far as your lane. Ruth bought Irwin a good pair of used skates last week at the auction. I know he's dying to use them. We'll meet you at the pond."

"I'll take you fishing on the ocean, if you want. There are charter boats going out of Lewes. I could hire a driver and—"

"I don't want to fish in the ocean, silly," she interrupted, touched that he would offer. "I'm happy just fishing for bass in your Dat's pond. You don't have to impress me."

"Not like John?"

"What I do with John on a date is one thing. What I do with you is another. Just be yourself, Charley. Don't act jealous and don't try to make me feel bad that I'm having fun with John. Just be my friend like you've always been…someone I can trust and tell my secrets to."

He kicked at a tuft of grass. He was wearing black leather high-tops and they looked new. In fact, his coat and blue shirt were new, as well. Charley looked especially fine on this Sunday morning. He'd shaved, and someone—probably his mother—had trimmed his hair.

"Do you have secrets, Miriam?" he asked.

"Not really. You know what I mean. I can tell you what I'm thinking. But if I did have secrets, I'd like to think that I could tell you."

"You can tell me anything. You ought to know that by now. I'd never judge you or think less of you, no matter what you say or do."

"Thank you. That means a lot to me."

They walked on, closer now, but not touching. Alone like this, it was more important than ever that they do nothing that would be considered improper. The trees were close on either side of the farm lane and the branches grew together overhead, forming an archway of light and shadow.

Birds fluttered overhead through the canopy of green leaves, calling to one another and singing cheerfully. From time to time, Miriam could catch a flash of scarlet or blue feathers as a cardinal or blue jay flew up at their approach. Miriam had walked this way dozens of times to Charley's house, but she'd never seen the woods so beautiful.

"Would you come early enough to share supper with us?" Charley asked after a few minutes. "Tomorrow, before we go fishing—you and Irwin. Mam will have plenty. She always does. Usually, on Monday, she makes a pot of vegetable soup to go with whatever is leftover from dinner."

Miriam hesitated. "Not yet, I think. If Irwin and I come to eat, everyone will think that you and I...that we've come to an agreement."

"Oh." He sounded disappointed.

"But I could pack a picnic and the three of us could eat at the pond." She smiled at him. "Before we start catching all those fish."

Charley nodded. "You're right. Mam would think it was settled and she'd start dropping hints about wedding dates. The picnic is a better idea."

"A lot simpler for both of us."

"It's what I am, what I'll always be," he said. "*Simple*. I work with my hands and try to follow God's laws as instructed by our faith and the *Ordnung*." He looked into her eyes. "But I'd promise to love you and care for you more than anybody else could. I want us to be together, to make a good Amish home, and God willing, I want us to have children together. Is that wrong, Miriam?"

She shook her head. "Not wrong, but it would be wrong if I didn't feel the same way about you. If we weren't right for each other."

"You know, I think I've always loved you."

"Charley, don't. Please. Let's keep it not so serious."

"But we're walking out together. This is when I'm supposed to tell you what I feel in my heart. Isn't it?"

"We're walking out to see if we're..." She stopped and then started again. "I know how I feel, but I don't know how to explain it."

"I think you love me, too, but you're just too stubborn to admit it."

"Charley, I—"

"What is this?" a deep voice demanded.

Miriam looked up to see Uncle Reuben standing in the path ahead of them. "We're not late for services, are we, Uncle?"

"Ne!" His expression was stern, his posture rigid. "You should not be here together without someone," he said. "It looks bad for young people to walk together without a chaperone. You know better."

"It's my fault," Charley said. "I walked over to the Yoders' this morning and asked Miriam to—"

"You and I will talk later." Uncle Reuben pointed toward Charley's house just visible through the trees. "Go and join the men. It is Miriam I wish to speak to."

Appearing uncertain, Charley glanced at her, then back at Uncle Reuben. "If she's in trouble, it's not her fault," he defended. "I'm not leaving her."

"Charley Byler. Are you questioning my authority?"

Charley shook his head. "No, Preacher Reuben. But we did nothing wrong and I wouldn't want you to think otherwise. I was just walking Miriam to service."

Her uncle frowned. "What I have to say to Miriam is private."

"Go on, Charley," Miriam urged. Her knees felt weak, but she knew she was innocent of any wrongdoing. "Please, Charley," she murmured. "It'll be all right. I've done nothing to be ashamed of."

Uncle Reuben motioned to Charley. "Go on now, before you make things worse."

Charley met her gaze, saw that she meant what she said and reluctantly walked away. When he was out of hearing range, her uncle took her hand in his.

"There is talk, Miriam, talk that worries me."

She blinked back tears. "Is this my uncle speaking to me, or my preacher?"

"Today," he said, "I speak to you as one of the shepherds of our faith. I have come, child, to deliver your first official warning from the bishop."

Chapter Fifteen

Miriam's stomach knotted as she stared at her uncle. He appeared so solemn in his good black coat and black felt hat. Usually, he looked like the other men in the community, but a bit Plainer. He wore his battered straw hat way into the fall, his old suspenders that had come apart and been knotted on the left side and worn blue trousers with patches on the knees. Not today. This morning, he looked the stern Amish preacher that the English liked to picture on their postcards.

Uncle Reuben was a serious man who rarely smiled, but his faded blue eyes were usually kind and his voice soft. Today, his tone was grating and she saw no kindness in his expression, nothing but disapproval and disappointment.

She was in trouble, *real* trouble. Among the Old Order Amish, the rule of the bishop and his two ministers was law. Their decisions on behavior in the community were absolute. If they decided that her behavior was loose, she could be placed under *meidung*. If she was shunned, she would be forbidden to enter the worship service... unable to sit at the same table with her family and friends.

Those she loved most might be forced to close their doors to her.

"What are you warning me about?" she managed, when she found her voice.

"You know what. Your behavior with the veterinarian."

"I don't know what behavior with John you're talking about," she protested.

"Bishop Atlee, Deacon Samuel and Preacher Perry have all mentioned your name to me this week. And what they said wasn't praiseworthy. It's my duty to tell you that you are treading on thin ice." He let go of her hand. "A witness told me that John Hartman dropped you off at your house last night, very late. And you were alone. This was not a trip in the middle of the day, as was the day you went to Easton which, as you know, was concern enough. But this is too much. Miriam Yoder does not ride in a car seated next to a man in the dark, unchaperoned."

"I *was* with John last night, but I *wasn't* alone. My sister was with me. He took us to Rehoboth Beach."

Her uncle studied her face. "I was told differently."

"By whom?"

"That's not important. What matters is your reputation and that of our community."

Miriam summoned all her courage. She had known there would be consequences to her decision to court two men at once and it was up to her to defend that decision. "Uncle Reuben, I have a right to know who is bearing false witness against me."

"Is it false?"

"Absolutely. Susanna was with us. You can ask my mother and sisters. Mam gave me permission to go to the boardwalk with John, but we had Susanna with us the whole time."

"Then why didn't your brother-in-law see Susanna in the cab of John's truck? Wilmer told me that he saw only the two of you, and you were sitting in the middle, beside John."

Miriam felt a flare of anger. Wilmer was spying on her? What other reason would he have had for being there that time of night? But she made herself remain calm. She nodded. "That's true, I *was* sitting beside him in his truck. But Susanna was there, too. She fell asleep. I had my arm around her and her head was in my lap. When we arrived home, Ruth and Anna met us at his truck. Susanna was so sleepy that they had to help her up the stairs to bed." She felt a quick surge of anger. "I can't believe Wilmer went to you with this. With…with false-hoods!"

"It was out of concern for your welfare and for that of your family. He means you only good, Miriam. With your father dead and your mother with no adult sons, your sister's husband might be considered the head of your family."

"Wilmer Detweiler?" She set her hands on her hips, her face flushing with anger that she fought again to keep out of her tone. "How can he take my father's place? He hardly ever walks through our door and he never speaks to any of us. Wilmer is a moody, mean-spirited man and if he went to you, it was to get me in trouble."

"Hush such talk," her uncle said. "Wilmer is a member of our church, husband to your own sister. Where is the charity in your heart?"

"Where's the charity in his?" She caught herself before she said more. It would be wrong to accuse Johanna's husband of being a bad father to his own children, or of Wilmer having an unkind reason for going to Reuben with this tale. She would be no better than he if she made such accusations.

He raised his hands, palm out. "Miriam."

"You're right," she said, lowering her gaze respectfully. "Perhaps my brother-in-law did mean the best for us. But he was mistaken. I wasn't alone with John last night. Not for a minute."

"I believe you," her uncle said after a moment. "But I must ask you, what is John to you? Have you thought what you may be risking, to associate so freely with a Mennonite?"

"Yes, Uncle, I have thought of it. And the truth is, I don't know how I feel about John. I'm trying to find out."

"So you *are* walking out with John?"

"I like him very much, Uncle Reuben. He's my friend." She tried to think before she spoke. "And…and if what I feel is more…"

"Then why are you allowing Charley to court you?"

She sighed. "It's complicated."

"It's wrong. It puts Charley in a bad light. You must decide if you want to be baptized and live according to the *Ordnung* or leave us and go out among the English. And know that if you do go, you will break your mother's heart, not to say that of your sisters and all those in Seven Poplars who love you."

"But I haven't yet been baptized." She gazed into his craggy face. "Shouldn't I see something of the world before I make the decision?"

Her uncle sighed. "The outside world is not as exciting as you might think." He glanced toward Charley's house. "Enough. We will be late. I will tell the bishop and the other elders that Wilmer was mistaken."

"So I'm not in danger of being punished?" Emotion caught in her throat. "Of being shunned?"

"Oh, child, where is your understanding? No one said anything of being shunned. Do you think that *meidung* is an act of punishment? One we would place on you lightly or without sufficient cause? Shunning is an act of love, Miriam, used only in the most extreme cases to save one of our own."

"And there are two warnings before shunning," she said. She looked up at him. "Is this still the first?"

"I think you should be more concerned about your attitude and not the legalities of your situation, but I see no reason to give you an official warning if Wilmer was mistaken. But as your uncle, I warn you to be more careful." He gestured toward the Byler house. "Go now and take your place among the women. It would not do to interrupt services on the Sabbath."

"Go without me, Uncle. I need a few minutes alone."

"You give me your word that you will come?"

She nodded. "I will. I need the peace of church right now more than ever."

Uncle Reuben hurried away and Miriam just stood there on the wooded lane, trying not to cry. How had she caused so much trouble for her family when all she wanted to do was to make the right choice for her future? She felt so confused, so…not in control.

"Miriam?" Charley stepped out from behind a wild rosebush not twenty feet away. "Are you all right?"

She blinked. "I thought you went—"

"I'm sorry, Miriam." He came to her and took her hands. "I started to do what he told me, but I couldn't leave you. I doubled back and hid in the trees. "You don't need to worry. I didn't hear what Preacher Reuben said to you, but—"

She pulled her hands out of his. "No, I want to tell you." She caught one bonnet string between her fingers and twisted it nervously. "Wilmer went to my uncle and accused me of going out with John alone, last night. It's not true." Quickly she explained that Susanna had been with her all evening. "And Uncle Reuben says that I'm being unfair to you because I've gone places with John and that people are talking."

Charley bristled, then pulled her close and hugged her. "They'd better not say it to me."

She laid her head on his shoulder for a long minute, feeling small and frightened in his arms.

He released her, stepped back and gazed into her eyes. "You're doing nothing wrong, Miriam. Take all the time you need. You know I love you and want you for my wife, but I want you to be certain that it's me you want. I don't want to be second-best, the man you were forced to marry to make everyone else happy."

"I'd never do that to you," she promised, rubbing her eyes. A few tears escaped down her cheeks and Charley handed her a new handkerchief from his pocket.

"Do you feel like going to church?" he asked. "If you don't want to, I'll stay with you. I could walk you home or—"

"I want to go to services. No matter how bad I feel, the hymns and listening to God's word always lift my spirits." She sniffed. "And if I didn't go, it would look like I'm ashamed—that I *have* something to hide."

He offered his hand again. "Then, let's go together."

She smiled, but tucked her hands behind her back. "Gladly, but there's no need to shock anyone. It *is* the Sabbath. And we'd better hurry, or we'll be late and we'll both be in hot water."

Side by side, they walked across the field to Charley's

mother's house, where the sounds of the first hymns were already sounding. "You go in through the kitchen," he suggested. "Your mother will think you've been helping out with the babies. I'll come from the front. Some of the younger guys are always sneaking in during the first hymn. No one will notice."

She laughed. "Wishful thinking. You and me both late? Everyone will notice."

He grinned at her. "It won't be the first time we've been in trouble, though, will it?"

"Hardly," she agreed. They were approaching the back of the farmyard. Rows of black buggies were lined up, but the horses had been turned into the pound or tied in the barn and sheds. Nothing was stirring but one gray tomcat and a bantam rooster.

"Before you go, I wanted to ask you something," Charley said as they reached the farmyard. "After church, this evening, could you take a ride with me—with one of your sisters, or *all of them?* Reuben can come, too, if he wants." He grinned and she grinned back. "I've got something I want you to look at."

"What is it?" she asked.

"You'll see. It's a surprise."

It was after seven o'clock that night when Hannah, Susanna, Charley and Miriam arrived at a home near Felton. Charley had hired a driver so that they wouldn't be out on the roads late in his father's buggy. It was evident to Miriam that the owners must be English, because the prefab house had a large satellite dish on the side lawn and an SUV and a pickup in the driveway.

"Tony works with me," Charley explained. "He knows that we use horses and he thought I might know someone who could help."

Puzzled, Miriam followed her mother and sister out of the van. The driver remained inside, listening to the radio, as Charley led the way to a white lean-to shed in the backyard. It had a Pennsylvania Dutch hex sign painted on the door and a fake weather vane on top. They were met by a man and a boy about six years old that Charley introduced as Tony and T.J. The little boy stared at them, but Miriam didn't mind. She knew that their Amish clothing must look as odd to T.J. as his red and yellow cartoon T-shirt and his short-cropped hair with the little rattail at the back appeared to Susanna.

"A fellow from the Air Force base boarded the pony here at my sister's for a few weeks," Tony explained as he opened the door to the shed. "Sherry loves animals and she can never pass up a sob story. The guy told her he rescued it from some trailer park and that it was temporary, her keepin' it, but then he must have been transferred or something because his phone was disconnected when she tried to call him when she didn't hear from him."

"Tony told me that the horse needed medical care," Charley explained to Miriam and her family.

"It's gentle enough to let kids crawl all over it." Tony walked in and switched on a ceiling light. "Sherry doesn't have the money to pay for a vet or to buy horse chow. This week she got a postcard from California. The guy who left the animal said sell it for what he owed her in board." He shook his head. "Sherry doesn't want to sell it. She feels sorry for it. She just wants to find the horse a good home."

Miriam wasn't listening anymore. Her attention was fixed on the ragged pony tied to a ring on the far wall. It was a brown and white pinto, standing about fourteen hands, with a dark mane and tail. Sadly, the animal appeared to be in terrible condition, ungroomed, hooves grown out, mane and tail tangled and so thin that her ribs showed.

"Poor *maedchen*," she crooned, going to the pony and stroking her neck. An empty bucket lay overturned on the concrete floor amid a few handfuls of what appeared to be corncobs and lawn clippings.

"Like I said." Tony sounded apologetic. "He needs a vet, but Sherry's a single mother with three kids and an ex that doesn't pay regular child support. She can't afford to take care of another stray."

Charley came to Miriam's side. "What do you think? Tony said Sherry told him the pony's trained to a carriage. With a little fattening up, she might make a good addition to your farm."

"It's a girl?" Tony bent and peered at the pony's underside. He was a big man with a bigger belly, bald, with the complexion of someone who'd spent a lifetime working outdoors. "Sherry thought it was a boy horse."

"It's a mare," Charley said, trying not to laugh.

Miriam checked the pony's teeth and then scratched behind her ears. She could see that the animal was young, no more than five or six years old, but her hooves were in terrible shape. Miriam couldn't tell if they'd ever been trimmed. They were cracked and so long that they curled up in the front. The pony was watching with huge brown eyes, eyes that seemed to be begging, *Help me. Please, get me out of here.*

Miriam picked up one of the pony's hooves, and then another. She ran her hands over the pinto's legs and felt the belly. Through it all, the animal stood patiently. Even the little mare's long coat was a disgrace. Tufts of hair were coming out and there was a bare spot on one hip. As Miriam inspected the raw skin closely, she saw telltale evidence of lice. She shuddered with distaste and quickly snatched her hand away.

Angry thoughts of what she would like to do to anyone who left a pony in this condition filled her, and when she turned to look at her mother, she could hardly speak. "Mam?"

Hannah nodded.

"You say your sister will let us have the pony for nothing?" Miriam turned to Tony. "Could we take her tonight?"

"Tonight?" The Englishman's eyes widened in surprise. "Sure, you can have her tonight, but we don't have a horse trailer."

She felt for the red cell phone in her pocket. "Lucky for us, we have a friend who does have a trailer."

"Ya," Charley agreed. "A friend of the family who happens to be a vet. So the pony will get good care."

"And a good home," Miriam said. "It's obvious that she needs it." She glanced at Charley. "Thank you," she murmured. "You're the best friend of all."

As September slipped into October and the trees turned from green to red and gold, Miriam's days and nights were filled to overflowing. With Molly and the new pony to care for, crops to get in and the usual farm chores, she was too exhausted to worry too much about her future or the possibility that she could still be banned for her *loose behavior*. Instead of worrying, she tried to take each day as it came, accepting God's simple pleasures around the farm.

The pony, named *Taffy* by Susanna, was already looking much better. Charley's brother Roland, a skilled farrier, had trimmed her hooves. John had given her a thorough medical examination and prescribed vitamins, a special horse feed, lots of grooming and medication for her infestation with lice. Because of Taffy's sweet disposition, Miriam guessed that the pony had suffered from the owner's ignorance and lack of care, rather than abuse. In any case, the entire family seemed delighted with her. Once Taffy regained her health, Miriam was certain that the little mare would make a dependable driving pony.

With Hannah's approval, Miriam continued seeing both John and Charley over the next three weeks. Always properly chaperoned, she walked to church with Charley, fished in his father's pond, went to husking bees and picked grapes and apples with him. Some evenings, Charley came by the Yoder farm and they played catch with a softball in the yard or a quiet game of cards with the family.

Dates with John were more exciting: the spaghetti supper at his uncle's church, lunch at a Mexican restaurant, a trip to the library, an afternoon movie at the mall and routine visits to care for ill or injured animals. Miriam took care never to do anything that her mother would consider inappropriate or that might bring censure from the church elders. If Miriam wasn't accompanied by one of her sisters, she took Irwin along.

On a Saturday in mid-October, Miriam and John were picking pumpkins at Samuel's farm when the two finally found a few minutes alone. Irwin had been helping, but he and Samuel's twins had gone off to join a softball game at the field beside the school. Technically, she and John were unchaperoned, but they were in a field in plain view for anyone who drove by to see, and therefore couldn't be accused of sneaking behind anyone's back to be alone.

Molly, recovered from her hoof infection and now pronounced by John as sound enough for light work, was hitched to the small cart. Eli had suggested that they sell decorated pumpkins for Halloween at his shop. Samuel had a bumper crop this year and was willing to let the Yoder girls have them for fifty cents each. It seemed a good idea that might bring in a little extra cash, so the whole family was helping out. John had come by to visit and was pressed into the pumpkin project. Miriam was in charge of the picking and Ruth, Susanna and Anna would do the painting.

Miriam was barefoot, her hair decently covered by a lavender scarf, as John lifted the pumpkins out of the muddy field and handed them up to her where she stood next to the cart. They already had more than a dozen in the vehicle when Miriam reached to take a particularly fat pumpkin with a long twisted stem. As she grabbed the pumpkin, her hand brushed John's and she blushed as she felt a jolt of excitement.

The pumpkin slipped out of her fingers, bounced off the low side of the cart and smashed on the ground. John grabbed her by the waist, lifted her into the air and set her down in front of him on the tailgate of the cart. Then, he leaned closer and kissed her.

"John!"

"What?" His eyes were sparkling.

"You…*we* can't do this." She pushed at his shoulders, putting a little distance between them.

"Why not?"

"Because…because you cannot be so familiar with me. We've talked about this. There can be no kissing."

"How about if I ask you to marry me?" He gazed into her eyes, a smile on his lips. "*Then* do I have a right to a kiss?"

Chapter Sixteen

"Marry?" Miriam's eyes widened. "You're asking me to marry you?"

He laughed. "That was the point of my courting you, right?"

She hadn't expected this. Not yet. Certainly not today. "And…and you're asking me now?"

"Why wouldn't I? You're special, Miriam. You're smart and funny and full of life. We'd be happy together—I know it. And…" He looked down at the ground, then up at her again. "And I think it's time we decided. We've seen enough of each other to know if this is what we want. I know it's what I want. And you'd have so much more freedom as a Mennonite."

She nodded, suddenly frightened and excited, at the same time. "It's a big decision," she heard herself say.

What was wrong with her? This was what she wanted, wasn't it? John was such a wonderful man, everything any woman would want in a husband: patient, gentle, hardworking. She could love him, if she didn't already. She could see herself having his children. But…*but what?* she wondered.

"Miriam?" His brow creased. "You're not saying

anything. A man asks you to marry him, you're supposed to…say something."

She let her hands fall to her lap. "I care for you so much," she said, "but the truth is, I don't know if I could abandon my faith…my family."

"You wouldn't be abandoning your family. You said yourself that if you become Mennonite, you'd still be welcome at your mother's table."

"But not church." She felt a sudden tightness in her chest. "If we were Mennonite, our children would not be welcome in the Amish church, either."

"We can figure it out. I'll do anything you want. I mean it." He pulled off his ball cap. "I'll become Amish, if that's what you want. How would I look in a straw hat?"

At first, she thought John was being silly, but she realized that beneath the joking, he was serious. "You would do that for me?" she murmured, gazing into his eyes. "You'd give up being a Mennonite? You'd become *Plain*, for me?"

"I would." He tossed his hat into the wagon. "As long as your bishop would give me some kind of exemption— so that I could continue my veterinary practice. I have to drive to care for my patients and I couldn't work in the clinic without electricity. But, maybe they could make an exception. I could be Amish at home and Mennonite in the world. I must not be the first man to do that."

"But your own faith, John, your family? How would they feel if you turned Amish?"

He shrugged, his handsome face growing serious. "What they want doesn't matter. I only care about us. I think you'd fit in well in the Mennonite life, but I mean it. I'll do whatever it takes to make you happy." He captured a loose lock of her hair that had escaped her scarf and wound it around his finger. "So will you marry me, Miriam Yoder? Will you be my wife?" He hesitated. "You're still not saying anything."

"I need time, John." She looked into his handsome, honest face. "I'm sorry, but I can't tell you this second. Can I have a few days?"

"Take all the time you need."

"All right," she promised, getting to her feet in the cart. She was trembling. He'd done it, asked her to marry him. She'd been so sure that if he did, when he did, that she'd say *yes*. He'd even offered to become Amish so she wouldn't have to leave her family or her church. So why hadn't the words come out of her mouth? Why hadn't she told him she would marry him? What was wrong with her? "I'll give you an answer soon."

"Tell me that you haven't made up your mind yet," he urged. "Tell me I still have a chance."

"You do," she said, smiling at him as she tossed his cap back and moved to the front of the cart. She unwound the leathers from the peg where she'd wrapped them and flicked the lines over Molly's back. "Walk on," she said.

She looked back, her heart full of love. John was still standing there with his hat in his hands, watching her. Her mouth still tingled from his kiss and her heart was racing. She could still feel the warmth of his touch.

Above, the sky was a brilliant blue, the clouds white drifting puffs of meringue. The air was rich with the scents of ripening pumpkins and fertile soil. *Please, God,* she prayed silently. *Help me to make the right decision. Help me find Your plan for me.*

It was Susanna who found Miriam later, sitting on the swing in the front yard, deep in thought. Susanna had smudges of white and green paint on her chin and nose, and a big streak down her skirt. Both chubby hands were covered in the poster paint that she'd used to decorate the pumpkins.

"Miriam!" Her little sister ran toward her, *kapp* strings flying. "Did you see Kitty-Cat? I want to show her my pun-kin."

Miriam wiped her eyes and smiled at her little sister. She didn't want Susanna to see that she'd been crying. Susanna's heart was so big that she could never bear to see anyone unhappy. She possessed a child's innocence, and a compassion that embraced every living thing. But Miriam couldn't explain her dilemma to Susanna. How could she expect Susanna to understand what she herself couldn't?

Miriam didn't know what to do. Two good men loved her and she couldn't decide between them. Worse, she'd let both of them kiss her and she'd liked it. What kind of Amish woman was she? Why couldn't she be as certain of her place in God's plan as Anna was? Why couldn't she make up her mind about something that should have been so simple? She didn't even have to choose between her faith and John's if she didn't want to. So, did she love John or did she love Charley?

Susanna came to stand in front of her. "What's wrong, Miriam?" She touched her cheek. "You sad?"

Miriam sniffed and nodded. She wished she had Charley's handkerchief. She knew she needed to blow her nose. She was afraid to speak. If she did, she was afraid she'd start crying all over again.

"Why?" A calico cat strolled out from under a lilac bush, elegant tail curved over her sleek back. "Kitty!" Susanna dove for her pet and returned with the purring cat in her arms. "I painted a pun-kin," she told the animal. "Want to see?"

"I think you painted Susanna," Miriam said, forcing a smile as she looked at her sister's paint-smudged face. Love for her little sister enveloped her like a hug. Susanna might be different from most people, but she brought joy to everyone around her.

"You want to see my pun-kin, Miriam?"

Miriam nodded. "In a little bit."

"You're sad," Susanna repeated. "Why are you sad?"

"I have a big decision to make, and it's hard."

"Mam says ask God. He knows."

"I have asked Him, Susanna," Miriam admitted. "Over and over, but I can't hear His answer."

"You have to listen. Mam says, 'Listen, Susanna. Open your ears.'"

The cat had curled up contentedly in Susanna's arms. "Do you pray?" Miriam asked.

Her sister nodded.

Miriam stroked the cat's head, and Kitty purred louder. "Why don't you go show Kitty the pumpkin you painted?"

Susanna tilted her head and patted Miriam's shoulder. "God loves you. Don't be sad."

Another tear trickled down Miriam's nose. "But I don't know what to do. I keep thinking and thinking, and I still don't know what's best."

Susanna's lips pursed and her brow furrowed in thought. Miriam could almost see the wheels turning, and she waited to see what would come out of Susanna's mouth.

"I think you should ask Charley."

"Ask Charley?" Miriam stared at her sister in confusion. She hadn't told her sister what decision she was trying to make.

"Ask Charley. He's smart. Not like me. He tells me things all the time when I don't know the answer."

It seemed to Miriam as if suddenly the clouds parted and the front lawn was bathed in warm, glowing sunlight. *Ask Charley? Ask Charley! Of course. That was the answer. Ask Charley.* She jumped up, threw her arms around Susanna and hugged her. "Don't ever think you're not smart! You are, Susanna. Thank you!"

"What?" Susanna demanded, but Miriam was already running toward the backyard.

Irwin's blue push-scooter was leaning against the porch. Miriam grabbed it and began to roll it toward the driveway. "Hey!" Irwin called. "Where you going with my scooter?"

"Just borrowing it!" Miriam shouted over her shoulder.

"Miriam!" Anna called from the front porch. "Where are you going?"

Susanna dashed around the house. "Charley's," she explained. "Miriam's going to ask Charley."

To Miriam's dismay, Charley wasn't home. His sister told her that Charley was at Roland's, laying block for a new chicken house. "Is something wrong?" Mary asked. "Do you need me to hitch up the buggy and drive you over?"

Miriam shook her head. "*Ne.* I'll be fine."

She turned and pushed the scooter back down the Bylers' lane and along the road past the schoolhouse. Cars and trucks whizzed past, and once an Amish horse and wagon rolled by and Lydia Beachy and two of her daughters waved.

"Hey, Miriam," Lydia called as she bounced a baby on her knee. "Would you like a ride?"

Miriam waved back, but shook her head. She didn't want to explain to Lydia or her girls why she was chasing Charley around the neighborhood. "I'm good," she said.

The Beachy buggy clattered past, little Elsie hanging half out the back door. Miriam was about to shout a warning, but then Verna yanked her back in and secured the door.

Miriam kept pushing the scooter and Susanna's words kept sounding in her head. *"Ask Charley. Charley's smart."* Maybe that was the answer. All she knew was that the despair that had smothered her for days had suddenly dissolved. Instead of sadness, she felt hope. One way or another, she had the feeling that everything would be settled once she found Charley. He knew her better than anyone. He'd tell her what to do.

By the time she got to Roland's lane, Miriam's leg ached from pushing the scooter, and she was hot and sticky. She stopped at the pitcher pump in the yard and pumped up a cup of cool water and then splashed her face to clean off the road dust. She left the scooter leaning against the pump and walked to the site of the new chicken house behind the barn.

Charley and Roland were both there, and Roland's two-year-old was with them. Someone had given Jared a big spoon and some plastic cups. The little boy was eagerly digging in a pile of sand, giggling and tossing sand in the air. An older neighbor, Shupp Troyer, was leaning on a stack of concrete blocks and giving advice on how the structure should be built.

"Charley, I need to talk to you," Miriam said, as soon as she greeted everyone. "Alone."

Charley exchanged glances with his brother, shrugged and finished tapping in the block he'd been laying. "Best see what she needs," he said to the two men. "Might be important."

As Charley walked away from the foundation, little Jared threw up his arms and squealed. "You want to come?" Charley swung the wiggling toddler up onto his shoulders. Jared giggled and grabbed hold of Charley's ears. "Easy on the ears," Charley protested. "I've only got two."

"You sure you want that trouble?" Roland called after them.

"*Ya.* He'll be fine," Charley assured him.

Charley was good with children. It seemed that they all loved him and he had immense patience with them. *He'll make a great father,* Miriam thought.

Nervously, she led the way back around the barn, past the calf pen, to a small pond beside a maple tree, with leaves already turning a brilliant red. The banks of the pond were thick with clover and Roland had built a high-backed bench on a small stretch of sand overlooking the water.

Heart in her throat, Miriam took a seat on the bench. Charley wrestled Jared off his shoulders, retrieved his straw hat and Jared's, and sat the little boy between them.

"What is it?" he asked.

Jared slid down off the bench and began to use his hat as a sand bucket.

"Jared, don't," Miriam said.

"*Ne,* let him be," Charley said. "It will keep him happy." He pointed to the water. "Stay here," he warned. "Don't get near the water or you'll have to go in the house with your mother."

Jared nodded and began digging a hole.

Charley looked at Miriam again and waited.

She folded her hands in her lap and stared at them. Her mouth was dry and her chest felt tight. She'd come this far; she couldn't let her nerve fail her now. "I need you to let me say what I have to say," she managed. "Don't say anything. Just hear me out first."

"All right," he agreed. The muscles in his face were taut, the expression in his eyes curious, but guarded.

"You know I've been thinking about you and John and which one I'm meant to be with. I've also been struggling with the decision to join the Amish church."

Charley nodded. "I do."

She swallowed. This was so difficult. She had to know the answer to her question, but she didn't want Charley to give the wrong answer. "I don't know too much about the Mennonite faith, but what I've learned seems good. What I wanted to ask you is if you've ever thought about not being baptized in *our* church?"

"Not join the Amish church?" Charley looked startled.

Jared began crawling toward the water, Charley snatched him up and put him back closer to the bench. "I mean it, Jared. Stay here, or back to the house and nap time."

Jared shook his head. "Na, na, na."

Miriam tried again. "What I meant was…would you be willing to turn Mennonite to marry me? If I wanted to become Mennonite?"

"You don't want to be Amish?" His mouth firmed.

She lifted a finger. "Please. Just listen."

Charley frowned, but he didn't say anything more.

"If we married and joined the Mennonite church, we could still live in Seven Poplars. You could keep your job, and we could see our families regularly. We could buy a truck and learn to drive it. We could go places. See things."

"This is what you want?" He glanced down at Jared and then back at her. He stared full into her eyes. "You want me to abandon the Amish church for a truck and a faster way of life?"

Jared began piling sand on Charley's high-top work shoe.

Miriam reached for Charley's hand. "I didn't *say* I wanted you to leave the church. Not that, exactly. I wanted to know if *you'd* stop being Amish if that was the only way I would agree to marry you."

Charley gripped her hand. When he spoke again, his voice was rough. "I love you, Miriam. I love you more than I love Roland or my sister or my mother, more than my own life. I want to make you my wife. I want us to have children together, but I want to raise them in our faith."

She held his gaze. "But what if leaving the Amish church is the only way I'd marry you?"

"If I had to stop being Amish to marry you…"

She waited, holding her breath for his answer.

He broke off, his voice ragged with emotion. "I can't do that, Miriam, not even for you." He shook his head. "I'm the same as I've always been. I'm a Plain man, like my father and grandfather, all the way back to the old country."

A maple leaf floated down, sailing past the bench to land on Jared's outstretched knee. "La-la-la," he squealed, grabbing the leaf with both hands.

Tears clouded Charley's blue eyes. "Ask me anything else, Miriam. Anything else I would do for you, but this is where I fit in God's world. I'm just good old Charley.

I'm not the kind of man who can change my faith, not even for you."

"You're certain?"

"From the bottom of my heart." He took a breath. "So if you want to be Mennonite, I wish you happiness with John."

Chapter Seventeen

Miriam smiled at him. "You mean that, don't you? You really mean you want me to be happy—even if it's with John?"

He nodded. "Of course. I love you. Why wouldn't I want you to be happy?"

The hurt in Charley's eyes was a raw wound. Miriam could feel her heart constricting. It had never occurred to her that both men might fall in love with her. And now, no matter which man she chose, she would have to refuse the other. How had she been so foolish as to let this go so far? Tears filled her eyes. "You say you love me, but do you trust me?"

His answer came all in a rush. "With my life."

She had to see John. *Now.* She had to tell him her decision. "Could you come with me to talk to John? I know it's a lot to ask, but I can only say this one time—and I need both of you to be there."

Charley picked up Jared, dusted off his clothing and adjusted the little boy's small hat. His gaze was on his nephew, not Miriam, as he said, "You're going to marry John and leave the faith?"

A rush of joy filled her, making her want to spin and

shout, to throw up her arms to the sky and laugh. "I didn't say that. I just said trust me, Charley. Now, come with me." Her tears were already fading. "Please."

"Do you know where John is? Is he at the office? We just can't go tearing around Dover chasing him in the buggy."

"*Ne.* I don't know, but I can find out."

Charley frowned as she pulled the red cell phone out of her apron pocket and pushed the button that would *speed dial* John's cell. Jared giggled and reached for the red phone with both chubby hands.

"Hello, John? It's Miriam." She took a breath and explained what she needed.

In seconds, she hung up and turned back to Charley and Jared. "He's at Hershberger's farm. Perry has a calf with a barbed wire cut. John offered to come here when he's finished tending the heifer, but I asked him to meet us at the schoolhouse. Halfway in between." She glanced around. "School's out for the day, and we can talk there in private."

Charley nodded. "I can drive you there." He shifted Jared to his shoulder. "But we'll have to bring this bundle of mischief with us. Roland needs to take Pauline to the doctor and I promised him I'd keep the boy until they got back."

"We can take him. No problem. And it will please Uncle Reuben that we have a chaperone." She chuckled. "Even if a small one."

Charley grinned at her. "*Ya.* You must set a good example for your sisters."

The tension seemed to ease between them as they walked back to where Charley had left his open buggy. There, Miriam lifted Jared into the seat while Charley went to tell his brother where they were taking the boy.

In just a few minutes, Charley returned to hitch his horse to the buggy. "Just as well Jared's going with us," he said. "Shupp wanted to know where we were off to and did your mother know."

Miriam chuckled. "Shupp is as bad as Aunt Martha. Such a gossip, he is."

Jared picked that moment to pull off his hat and sent it flying.

Charley retrieved the boy's straw hat, climbed up into the seat and gathered the leathers in one callused hand. "You sure you know what you're doing?" he asked Miriam as he passed Jared's hat to her. "You won't regret what you've decided?"

She smiled at him over Jared's head. "Never." She smoothed back the toddler's hair and placed the hat on his head.

"Keep your hat on," Charley ordered as he drove out of the barnyard. "Just like Dat does."

As they passed the house, Pauline waved from an open upstairs window. "Look," Miriam pointed. "There's your Mam."

Jared giggled, bounced up and down and waved with both hands.

Neither Miriam nor Charley spoke as he guided the horse out of the lane and onto the blacktop road. A tractor trailer and a line of cars passed, but Charley paid them no mind. He kept the gelding at a fast trot and didn't pull off onto the shoulder until a convertible ran up on them and blew the horn.

Jared's face paled and his lower lip came out. It appeared that he was about to burst into tears until Charley took him onto his lap and let him hold the ends of the reins. "Shh, shh," Charley soothed. "This is a good horse. He's not scared of the cars and you shouldn't be, either."

Jared sniffed and clung tight to the leathers.

"What a big boy you are," Miriam encouraged. "Your Dat will be proud of you."

As they passed the chair shop, they saw Eli and Ruth standing outside the front door and waved. "Eli's making her a walnut table as a wedding gift," Miriam said. "Roman's giving them two chairs to match it, but it's a surprise."

Charley nodded. "It will be a happy day, their wedding. I hope your sisters can come home to share in Ruth's joy."

"*Ya.* They will. Aunt Martha and Dorcas have promised to go out and stay with *Grossmama* for the week so Leah and Rebecca can be here."

Charley looked dubious. "That doesn't sound like Martha."

Miriam smiled. "She's a good woman, Charley. Sometimes, it's hard for her to show it. But she knows how important it is to Mam to have us all here for Ruth's wedding." She grasped the railing as Charley reined the horse across the intersection and turned onto the road that led to the schoolhouse.

"It goes to show, you shouldn't make hasty judgments," Miriam said. "Even when it comes to Aunt Martha."

"*Ya,*" Charley agreed. "I suppose it does." He hesitated. "I've been taking instruction from Preacher Perry, for my baptism. I didn't say anything to you before, but…"

"So you are definitely going to join the church?" she asked. "There's no chance you would change your mind?"

He shook his head. "Not even for you."

She took a deep breath and stared out at the fields of corn on either side of the road. These were English farms. Soon a giant combine would roar down the rows and harvest the corn…while at the Byler place and many others, it would be Amish men cutting the corn stalks with machetes and stacking them in shocks. It was as though the Amish were caught in a previous time, she thought. Everything we do is the old way, following tradition, even if it means more work. But, she had to admit, the rows of corn shocks stretching across the fields made for a beautiful sight.

John's truck was parked beside the schoolhouse. Charley guided the horse into the drive and up to the hitching rail. Miriam climbed down and reached up for Jared.

"Swing!" he cried, pointing. "Swing!"

"I'll take him," Charley offered as he tied the gelding to the post.

"Later," Miriam said. Holding Jared by the hand, she walked over to where John waited by the pickup.

"Who have you got here?" John asked.

While Miriam made the introductions, John opened the glove box and took out a package of pretzel sticks. "Okay?" he asked, before offering the little boy a pretzel. Miriam nodded, and Jared plopped down on the grass with a pretzel in both hands and a smile on his face.

John looked from Miriam to Charley. "I guess this is serious," he said.

Miriam's courage wavered. This was so hard. How could she say what had to be said? How could she make them understand how she felt without hurting either John or Charley?

"I think she's made up her mind," Charley said, coming to stand beside Miriam. He crossed his arms over his chest. "I want to wish you both—"

"Charley Byler, will you hush and let me say my piece," Miriam blurted.

Then John started to speak and she held up a hand. "That goes for you, too, John Hartman." She felt a little light-headed and wished she was at home milking the cows, or even peeling potatoes, anywhere but here.

Miriam took a deep breath. "I want you to know, I love you both," she said softly. She looked at one man and then the other. "John, you have opened new windows to the world for me. And, Charley...Charley, you've always been my best friend."

Charley and John looked at each other and then back at her. They both looked nervous.

Heat flushed under Miriam's skin; she was shaking inside. What if she messed this up? What if she lost both of them in the telling?

It didn't matter. She had to be honest, to them and to herself. "If I have hurt either of you, I'm sorry from the bottom of my heart. I mean that. I never meant to hurt anyone."

"I just want you to be happy," Charley said. He picked up Jared and cradled the boy against his chest. "That's what's important, Miriam. I'll always be your friend, if you'll let me."

She smiled at him. "I hope you will. I hope we'll always be best friends." Then she turned and reached for John's hand, and his face lit with an inner flame.

"Miriam..." John murmured.

She placed the red cell phone in his palm and closed his fingers around it. "This belongs to *your* world," she murmured. "It was kind of you to lend it to me, but I don't need it anymore." She moved to stand beside Charley and Jared. "I love you, John, but as a dear, dear friend, not as a husband."

John nodded. "You're going to marry Charley, after all."

"I love him, and he and I are meant to be husband and wife," she answered. "I realized that when Charley told me that he couldn't change his faith, not even for me. You're a good man, John, but my husband must be a man of strong faith. His love for God must be stronger than his love for me."

"I think I understand." John hung his head as he slipped the red cell back into his pocket, but then he looked up again. "But I still want to be your friend...and Charley's, if he'll let me."

But she wasn't listening. She was gazing up into Charley's eyes. "If he'll have me after I've been so foolish."

"Me?" Charley croaked. "You want *me?*"

John cleared his throat and reached for Jared. "Let me take this little guy," he said hoarsely. "Give you two a minute alone." He turned his attention to Jared. "Would you like to blow the truck horn?" he asked the toddler, tickling his belly.

"Beep! Beep!" Jared shouted with a giggle.

Charley stood staring at her as John walked away. "Me?" he repeated.

"*Ya,* you." She was crying, tears flowing, her lower lip quivering. "Will you marry me, Charley?"

He didn't move a muscle. She wasn't sure that he was breathing. "When?" he asked.

She let out a great sigh of relief, smiling through her tears. "Um...I don't know." His question took her by surprise. "We've got to join the church first. Be...be baptized."

"When?" he repeated.

She threw her arms around him. "Weddings are in

November, you great ox. Will you marry me in November?"

His arms closed around her in a hug so tight that it took her breath away. *"Ya,"* he agreed. "In the Amish faith I will make you my wife, as soon as the bishop will allow. And all my life I will love you, Miriam Yoder… every day. And every day, I will thank God for you."

On the second Thursday of November, the Yoder house overflowed with guests—not only Bishop Atlee and the ministers and deacon of their church but two visiting bishops and three additional ministers from Pennsylvania. Hannah was everywhere, bustling about, directing the setup of chairs for the church service and the last-minute preparations and storage of food in the kitchen. Assisting her were her daughters: Anna, Susanna, Johanna, Leah and Rebecca and her best friend Lydia. Already, men and women were taking their places for the ceremony and the first stanzas of the opening hymns were spilling through the windows and doors into the yard. Upstairs, the two couples had spent the last hour and a half in council with the bishops and ministers.

At ten minutes past nine, by the tall case clock on the stair landing, Samuel came down the steps. Immediately, those who were still milling around took that as a signal to be seated. "Hannah, it's time," Samuel called from the bottom of the steps. "You don't want to be late to your own daughters' wedding, do you?"

Cheeks flushed, Hannah brushed back a stray strand of hair, smoothed her apron and hurried to take her place in the rows of chairs. Samuel winked at her as he crossed the aisle. "It will be fine," he mouthed silently, and took up the hymn with the others once he'd reached the men's section.

Hannah was too nervous to utter a sound. She fumbled with her hymn book, found the page and then lost it. Rebecca, with Susanna in tow, took a chair to Hannah's right, took the book and found the correct page for her mother. Anna, Leah and Johanna moved quietly into seats behind them as the bishops and ministers came down the stairs and entered the ministers' row.

"Here they come," Rebecca whispered.

Heads turned and waves of whispers flowed under the words of the hymn as Ruth and Eli came down the stairs hand in hand. Ruth's dress and cape were the blue of Susanna's eyes, and the depth of her smile brought a tear to Hannah's eye. Behind them, equally as solemn and equally as beautiful came Charley and Miriam. Her younger daughter had chosen a deeper shade of blue, more summer sky than her sister's clothing. Both wore crisp white *kapps,* the symbol of their reverence before God.

Rebecca squeezed Hannah's hand. "They look happy," she whispered.

"*Ya.* Happy." Hannah found her voice and took up the words of the old song of praise for God's blessings.

The two couples took their places in the front row. Miriam clasped Ruth's hand and leaned close. "Scared?"

"*Ya.* You?"

Miriam glanced up at Charley. How handsome he looked in his black coat and vest, how solid. She shook her head. "Not with Charley," she murmured.

Charley looked down at Miriam and smiled. "I love you," he murmured as Bishop Atlee cleared his throat to begin his sermon.

"I love you, too," Miriam breathed. "From the bottom of my heart. Forever."

Epilogue

Winter...

Charley opened the inner stairway door and stepped into the spacious finished attic that ran the length of Ruth and Eli's new house. Both hands were full and Miriam hurried to take the mugs of hot cocoa before he spilled them.

"How's the geometry going?" he asked as he placed the plate containing two slices of apple pie on the table that divided the bedroom area of their apartment from the living area.

"Almost done." Miriam pointed to her desk. "Two problems to go." She eyed the pie. "I suppose I could take a break."

"*Ya,*" he agreed. "So the cocoa doesn't get cold." He glanced around the single room. "The curtains look nice. You must have put them up today while I was at work."

Miriam sighed. "Ruth did. Anna finished sewing them while I was cleaning the stalls." The curtains did look nice. They were simple white cotton, identical to those in her mother's house and exactly the same as the ones on Ruth's windows on the floor below, but they set off the paneled pine walls and the blue denim covering Mam had sewn for her couch and Charley's easy chair.

She loved their new home, not under Mam's roof as Charley had suggested, but under Ruth and Eli's. They had the big finished attic that would someday, God willing, offer bedrooms for a large family of children. For now, it was perfect for her and Charley. She could remain on the home farm, continue caring for the animals and putting in crops, and she and Charley could have the privacy that any newly married couple wanted. To make the arrangement even better, Eli, Charley, Irwin and Roland had spent two Saturdays adding an outside staircase so Miriam and Charley didn't have to walk through Ruth's kitchen to get in and out.

Charley had plans to add a small kitchen in the front of the open room, but she didn't care when. Cooking had never been one of her better skills. As it was, they ate breakfast with Ruth and dinner and supper at Mam's. To balance out the living arrangement, Charley paid rent and Miriam cared for Taffy, a wedding gift to Eli and Ruth.

Charley settled into his comfortable chair, set his cocoa on a table and motioned to her. "Come sit here, with me."

Miriam smiled. This had become a habit with them at the end of the day. She'd cuddle up in his lap and they'd talk, tease or just enjoy being close and warm. She liked being married and she especially liked being married to Charley. So many exciting things had happened in the months since they'd taken their vows together.

A delay in the hospital construction had given them three weeks to travel west to visit friends and distant relatives. Together, they had ridden a steam train to an old mining camp in Colorado, stared in awe at the Grand Canyon in Arizona and waded in the Gulf of Mexico in

Texas. So many new sights and sounds, so many memories to cherish… And best of all, when they'd returned to Delaware, Charley had surprised her with the best wedding gift she could imagine.

He'd gotten permission from Bishop Atlee, Uncle Reuben and Preacher Perry for her to continue her education by mail. She could get her high school diploma and some college from a Christian school so that she would be fully qualified to teach at the Seven Poplars' School if her mother chose to retire the post. It was the most wonderful gift anyone could have given her.

Charley held out his arms and Miriam went into them. As always, she felt safe and happy. Charley was everything any Amish girl could want in a husband and he'd promised her that they would make decisions together in their new family.

She curled up and laid her head on his chest. He smelled good, better even than the cocoa with marshmallows on top that he'd brought upstairs. "Have I told you how much I love you, Charley Byler?" she teased.

"Not in the last hour."

"I do."

"Do what?"

She giggled as she stroked his bristly chin. As a married man, Charley was expected to grow a beard. His was somewhat reluctant to grow anything resembling Samuel's neatly trimmed and lush beard and all the men teased him about it. "I love you, husband." She waited.

Charley didn't say anything.

"Well?" she demanded.

"Well what?"

"Do you have something to say to me?"

"It's snowing out. Big flakes. We should be able to build a snowman tomorrow."

"Snowing?"

"*Ya.* Cold, white, frozen water. You know, *snow.*"

When she listened, she could hear the howl of the winter wind and imagine the snow falling. It made their home seem all the more a perfect nest, high in the trees, safe from the world. "Are you sorry you chose me, Charley?"

"Are you sorry you didn't pick that fancy Mennonite boy with the ball cap and the pickup truck?" He tickled her until she squealed with laughter. "Tell the truth," he said.

"*Ne. Ne.*" She wrapped her arms around his neck and kissed him tenderly. "Only you, Charley. You are the only man for me...the only husband. I was just too blind to see it."

"Not as blind as me or I would have made my move long before that city boy caught sight of you." He kissed her again. "I love you, Miriam. And I thank God every day for giving you to me."

"It's like Susanna said," Miriam said. "We have to listen if we want to know God's plan for us. Not just pray for an answer, but listen."

"Have I told you that I love you?" he teased.

"Not in the last thirty seconds."

"I could tell you every thirty seconds for the rest of our lives."

She giggled. "Our cocoa would get cold."

"Then we'll have to drink it cold, I suppose," he said. "With the pie."

"Oh, I forgot the pie."

"Pie later, kissing first."

"Whatever you say, Charley." He kissed her again and sweet sensations danced from the tip of her nose to the soles of her feet.

"Just remember that," he murmured. *"Whatever you say, Charley.* You keep saying that, and we'll never have a disagreement."

"Yes, husband," she said meekly, then tugged at his chin whiskers.

"Ouch."

"Just so you remember your promise. We decide together."

"To kiss or eat pie?"

"Maybe both."

"Ya," he agreed. "Both is good. But each in its own time." And he leaned over and blew out the lamp.

* * * * *

Dear Reader,

I invite you to join me in rural Delaware in the world of the Old Order Amish as we continue along our journey with Hannah Yoder and her daughters. Like so many choices, Miriam's will not be an easy one. It's never difficult to make a decision when one choice is good and the other is bad, but what if both choices are equally good ones? How do we know what God's plan is for us? How do we know who to choose when it comes to love and marriage?

Miriam and Charley Byler have been best friends since childhood; everyone in Seven Poplars assumes they will marry. But then, Mennonite John Hartman comes along and offers her the possibility of a life outside the Old Order Amish Church, a life of excitement and new places and experiences. How will Miriam choose?

I hope that you will come back and join me in Seven Poplars when Miriam's twin, Anna, learns that a man in her life has been watching her for a very long time and will make her an offer she can't refuse. Or can she?

Wishing you peace and joy,

Emma Miller

QUESTIONS FOR DISCUSSION

1. Miriam was interested in John Hartman from the first day she met him. Knowing he was not of her faith and knowing her family would not approve of him as a suitor, do you think Miriam should have pursued her interest in John? Do you think two people must be of the same faith to have a successful marriage? What are the advantages of same faith marriages? Are there disadvantages? If so, what?

2. Charley says he has loved Miriam since they were children. Do you think it's possible for a childhood infatuation to blossom into a love that can sustain a marriage? What are the advantages of marrying someone you've known since you were a child? The disadvantages?

3. Miriam's family seems to think that Charley is the man for her. Arranged marriages have been made since the beginning of time, and are still prevalent today in some cultures. Do you think family members can choose a partner for a loved one, resulting in a successful marriage?

4. The Old Order Amish do not believe in higher education. Do you think this is good for their community? Do you think it's good for the individual? Do you think families will branch off into new orders some day, in order to allow further education for their members?

5. The subject of Mam remarrying is mentioned several times in *Miriam's Heart* (and in the previous book

in the series, *Courting Ruth*). Do you think Mam should remarry, as is expected by her community? How do you think this will affect her? Her family?

6. Both John and Charley are good men. Why do you think God sometimes places two choices before us, both good, but only one that is right? Can you think of an instance in your life when you had to make a choice, but both were good options?

7. Do you think it's fair to Charley and John that Miriam chooses to court both of them at the same time? Do you think both men would be happy with Miriam or do you foresee problems between John and Miriam? Charley and Miriam?

8. When you heard that *Grossmama* was not doing well in Ohio, and that Leah and Rebecca are having an increasingly difficult time taking care of her and Aunt Jezebel, what was your reaction? Do you think Hannah should be taking on this problem, especially considering the fact that *Grossmama* has made it plain that she doesn't care for Hannah? What would you do in Hannah's shoes?

9. As the courting progresses between Miriam and Charley and Miriam and John, who did you see her better suited to? In her position, who would you have chosen? Who do you think Miriam should marry?

10. Do you think Miriam chose the right man to be her husband? Why or why not?